The Identity
of
Max Sledge

C. Marcus Parr

Et Cetera Press
2009

C. Marcus Parr

This is a work of fiction. Names, characters, places and incidents are either the product of the author's imagination or are used fictitiously.
Any resemblance to actual events or locales or persons, living or dead, is entirely coincidental. The author's purposeful use of names of actual events, locales, or persons, living or dead, is incidental to the plot, and is not intended to change the fictional character of the work.

DESIGNED BY C. MARCUS PARR
Set in Garamond

et

Published by Et Cetera Press
Sandy, OR 97055
www.lulu.com/content/4894348

Author's Note
Unless otherwise attributed,
the author composed all prose herein.

ISBN 978-0-578-00678-9
1. Travel—Atlantic Crossing—Europe—Italy—Greece—Amsterdam—Fiction. 2. Middle-aged men—Mystery writers—Fiction. 3. Fraud—Interpol—Crime Fiction—Romance.

Printed in the United States of America

For Leslie Ann, always

C. Marcus Parr

Chapter One

NEW YORK HARBOR tugboats pushed the transatlantic ocean liner Northern Star from her berth at Pier 92. A muscular tug named the Margaret Moran nudged the great ship like a bulldog, and Bob Dunn stood at the rail to watch. Other first class passengers, dressed in pastels and soft cottons, waved and tossed streamers to well wishers on the pier. *"Bon voyage. Bon voyage!"* After the ship was underway, Bob Dunn returned to his suite.

He begged off the customary launch parties and ordered room service instead. A young man in a white short coat brought a bottle of Mouton Champagne with an accompaniment of caviar and canapés. Dunn reclined in a chaise lounge and drank from a fluted glass while he read Proust, looking up occasionally at the gray loneliness of the Atlantic.

He had reached that age when most of life seemed to have passed him by. Looking back on his divorce, so long ago, he regretted an inconsequential faux pas that had grown in significance. The champagne softened his laments and kindled the memory of a few romantic interludes that he enlarged upon. He did not miss his wife so much as he missed companionship.

He returned his attention to Proust. He saw how *Remembrance of Things Past* treated time as both destructive and positive forces in life. Perhaps, he thought, the Master's intuitive memory will rub off on me. Now he had the time to observe. He wanted to learn from Proust's methods, which involved examining the details of a person's maturity and recording it faithfully, something he had failed at in his own work. The transatlantic crossing was meant to cure the worst writer's block of his career. His agent had told him, "The cruise will give you time, Bobby, to observe others and invent something new." Out of these resources he would create more believable characters for future Max Sledge Mysteries, Bob Dunn's series of modestly successful novels written under the penname Ashley Winslow.

He doubted his agent's counsel. This was no simple writer's block. It was more like an iceberg than something easily resolved by a cruise. Lately, Dunn had the feeling that his muse had died. No ocean crossing or first class accommodations could ever be expected to resurrect what he'd lost so long ago.

Getting up for a refill, he pressed his ear to the wall and heard the laughter of women and the clinking of cocktail glasses. He indulged a cigarette and mulled over the past. He chased after a thousand second thoughts of what he should have done differently in life. Eventually, he grew maudlin and wept into a cocktail napkin.

"How did Marcel do it?"

On that first night at sea, he slept fitfully in the slumber of the inebriate. By morning, the weather turned ugly. As if to defy assurances in the brochure that she was the most seaworthy ship of the Cunard line, the Northern Star pitched and yawed like a cork on the high seas. By noon, Dunn managed to go on-decks and take lunch alone, although he had little appetite. For the most part, the promenade was abandoned. Most passengers preferred to suffer seasickness and hangovers below, in private quarters of this ghost ship.

On deck he did what he had fancied himself doing in the many years of planning the crossing. He read books that he'd been meaning to read his entire life. He read while inclined on a chaise in a wool blanket while a smart-looking waiter served espressos. After lunching on a bagel with cream cheese, capers and lox, Dunn requested a demitasse and decanter of their finest brandy along with more canapés. The hair of the dog soothed him into a languid afternoon and evening. The briny air and ocean churned by the onrushing ship invigorated Dunn. He remarked to a complete stranger that he had never felt more alive.

Either the sea air or the brandy was chipping away at his writer's block. The root of his difficulty, he realized, was his penchant for creating two-dimensional characters in a three-dimensional plot. Even Max Sledge, the anchor in the series, was a cliché. He resolved to carefully observe human behavior during the crossing and record it faithfully as Proust had done, and then perhaps "invent something new."

By the late afternoon, the sea had settled into a luxuriant calm which drew passengers out of their cubbyholes. At sunset when the dinner bell was rung, the Atlantic resembled a dimpled sheet of antique glass. Dining was strictly black tie. In the main hall, the Polaris Room, Dunn met others from the first class section as he made the rounds of introductions before being seated.

He introduced himself as "Ashley Winslow," his pseudonym. "Call me Ash."

"And what do you do for a living, Mr. Ash?" came the frivolous voice of a frivolous-looking woman.

"I'm a novelist."

"Oh," the woman cooed and flashed her heavy mascara. "Could I have read anything of yours?"

"I wouldn't have a clue," Dunn said.

It was liberating to be called Ash. His was a tepid fame, hardly worth the effort he'd taken to write dozens of books; the kind of celebrity that brought more embarrassment and trouble than it was worth. He suffered the inconveniences of success without enjoying its benefits. He often wished never to have invented the sleuth Max Sledge, or to have published a word under a pseudonym. He would have been happy to die in obscurity with the palindrome of *Bob*. But on the cruise, this once-in-a-lifetime event, he left behind the old life with an eye to starting afresh. Onboard he could observe behavior like a scientist, and people would call him Ash, that man of mystery; a loner with a certain *je ne sais quoi.*

Among the dinner party were Dr. and Mrs. Paulson, a monumentally boring couple. Edie Paulson—the frivolous woman who'd made the earlier remark about his books—was a class-sensitive female who dropped the names of celebrities she had met or offhand seen onboard. She began sentences with "My dear, let me inform you…" with a fake lilt to throw Dunn off her New Jersey upbringing. She referred to her husband as "Dr. Paulson," never by first name. The *doctor* was a chiropractor.

Dunn shook the hands of Frank Whitten, a widower, who traveled with his only daughter whose name was mumbled in passing and immediately forgotten. The Unnamed Daughter was painfully shy. She was a librarian with unplucked eyebrows and an aversion to makeup. After dinner, Whitten confided in Dunn over a nightcap, "I hope the cruise sparks romance for Melissa."

Dunn nodded to himself and smiled. He thought Melissa's chances for romance were as poor as his own.

The sixth seat at the table remained empty throughout the first three courses of squab in a lentil sauce, lobster bisque, fresh greens, and an excellent selection of wines poured by the sommelier. While dessert was served, an older lady joined their party and begged their indulgence for being late. Miss Surmelian had undergone plastic surgery as a poor substitute for the fountain of youth. Her features were frozen in perpetual surprise. When Dunn shook her hand it was like shaking the hand of a perfumed mummy. In his notebook he jotted a line about perfumed mummies and plastic surgery, aspects to remember for the next Max Sledge Mystery.

Dr. Paulson tried to raise everyone's ire by bringing up politics. He got no takers, not on an Atlantic crossing, not when passengers sought relaxation and enjoyment. Whitten proved a marvelous teller of humorous stories, most of which were slightly off-color or at the expense of illegal immigrants.

Conversation was deflated when Miss Surmelian mentioned something about her nerves. "I hate the ocean," she said. To put her mind at ease, Dunn mentioned that the Northern Star sailed specifically during the fall and winter because of her stability. "During summer months she's pressed into cruise service," he said. When Dunn asked what Miss Surmelian was worried about, she whispered, "*Titanic*. Did you see the movie?"

Dunn assured her that the British flagship of the White Star Line, all forty-six thousand gross tons of her, was not the Northern Star. Everyone at the table knew the story of the maiden voyage from Southampton to New York, where the Titanic struck an iceberg about one hundred miles from Grand Banks just before midnight on April 14, 1912. Of the twenty-two hundred people aboard, fifteen hundred had died. "The American millionaires John Jacob Astor and Benjamin Guggenheim were lost at sea,"

Dunn remarked. Miss Surmelian shuddered. "It sank because of flawed steel plate and poor rivets. I can assure you, we're safe aboard this vessel. She's proven herself seaworthy." In almost a whisper, he said to her, "The Captain's given me his personal assurances we won't sail anywhere near the iceberg fields."

Later, when Miss Surmelian joined Edie Paulson on a trip to the Ladies, Dunn did his level best to engage Whitten's daughter Melissa to no avail. She finally responded to his simple prompts, but she spoke so softly he did not hear her above the salon's hubbub.

He passed the next day alone and overwrought. The writer's block persisted. On that first day out, it had been the brandy more than anything that had improved his outlook. Now that he was sober, his laptop sat idle as he followed a routine of reading, eating and sleeping until the afternoon when he ran into—quite literally—a young woman at the health spa. As he crossed the jogging track for the steam room, wearing a terrycloth bathrobe, his nose stuck in Proust, a thirty-something in Spandex ran smack into him, knocking them both down. She was apologetic although it was entirely Dunn's fault—and he told her so.

They disentangled their limbs, and Dunn helped the young woman to her feet. "No broken bones, I hope," he said with a fatherly smile.

"I am *so* sorry." She gave an emphatic apology. "Are you all right?"

In his best Ashley Winslow, he said, "Don't worry. I have no-fault insurance."

She laughed.

As a show of good faith, he offered to buy a cup of espresso or a smoothie, whatever she fancied, at the Spa Bar. To his utter astonishment, she accepted.

They sat side by side, he in a bathrobe and feeling a bit exposed, and she in spandex shorts and tank top. She ordered a smoothie, and Dunn an espresso.

"Call me Ash," he said.

Her name was Audrey Klein; a Jewish father, mother Native American, she was quick to add. She was from a little town in Kentucky that Dunn had never heard of. She expressed a smidge of a regional brogue through certain words requiring a softer vowel. The nuance demonstrated a failure of many elocution classes taken to improve her diction. Audrey claimed to be a television news anchor for a local New York City NBC affiliate. "I've done some news reading on weekends with MSNBC," she said, suggesting that Dunn might have seen one of her shows. He explained that he didn't have cable or a satellite dish and therefore could not have watched her on TV. She was taken aback as though being disconnected from mass communications was more appalling than Original Sin.

"Where do you live?" she asked, as if to imply that he must live in the outermost reaches of civilization. "Zambia? Or Mongolia?"

Dunn embellished his circumstances by making Max Sledge's life his own. He did not mention his cramped townhouse on the outskirts of suburban Vacaville, California, the epitome of Generica with its strip malls and car dealerships, of Anywhere, USA. He said nothing of a life lived through loneliness and regret. Instead, he lied that he owned an Oregon farm (an unrealized dream). "I live in the restored mansion of a failed northwest lumber baron. It's about as pastoral a setting as you can get. Creeks and hayfields, its where I write my books, in a gabled attic. Perhaps you've read something of mine?" he asked, although she had not. She said that she did not read very much because work on television kept her busy.

Dunn dreamed up the story that he had planted a vineyard on the farm from which he produced a fine pinot noir, all of it a bald-faced lie. She was fascinated, and Dunn smitten, this being a cruise and she the first person with whom he'd come into contact that talked about something other than stock portfolios. They made repeated promises to say hello should they "run into one another again," and they went their separate ways, she to the showers and Dunn to the steams.

He thought that this would be the last of it, but he saw her again in the evening before dinner. Audrey sidled up, looking radiant. She glowed in a lavender cocktail dress offset by a string of pearls. He hardly recognized her. At the spa he could see that she possessed natural beauty, but he was quite unprepared for her radiance. The perfect female form. Her lively banter put him completely off the hors d'oeuvres and complimentary champagne—she spoke at such a pace, Dunn could not keep up—until the second dinner bell when she insisted that he join their table. He accepted. He had no choice, she assured him.

In comparison to his mandatory dining companions in first class, Audrey's thirty-something friends were vigorous, enthusiastic people, not automatons or consumerists or advertisements for plastic surgery clinics. There was Bill and Ned, a gay couple from San Francisco, who had made it big in the catering business. They were delightful and entertaining conversationalists, glib and unabashed. For his austere looks and saber wit, Bill could easily have passed for a tanned Oscar Wilde or acted the part in one of those famous writer biographies on PBS.

Dunn meet Gene and Sally Seabrook who hailed from Ann Arbor, Michigan, Gene having made good as an insurance claims adjuster, one of those inexplicable jobs people do in anonymous office buildings. Gene spoke in a forthright voice as the proud graduate at the top of his class of an obscure Midwest college. Dunn enjoyed Sally's warmth and charm, and Gene did seem genuinely glad for his joining their party. The Seabrook's stood on the cusp of middle age but denied their galloping maturity through trendy clothes and haircuts more suitable to someone much younger. As with some people of a certain age, the Seabrook's refused to submit to the clock.

Then there was what Dunn presumed to be another married couple, Stanley Gray and his significant other, Hollis. Of everyone seated at table, he least liked Stanley Gray. He reminded Dunn of a seismograph, sensitive to the slightest vibration. Right out of a supermarket thriller with stereotypic acne scars and guarded eyes; a low level bureaucrat from a Balkan country who has grown weary of stamping passports. When he shook Dunn's hand, he did not look him in the eye or smile. His breath stank of cigarette residue overruled by aftershave. It seemed implicit that Hollis was Mrs. Stanley Gray by their familiarity. Dunn had to wonder what a lovely young woman saw in the *apparatchik*.

He said, "You and your husband must be enjoying the cruise, now that we have smoother sailing?"

Hollis assured him that she wasn't married, another faux pas on Dunn's part. Audrey stepped in to save him by introducing her friend. "Hollis McAllister, of the *Boston McAllister's*...?" she said, as though Dunn should know. Audrey-of-the-tight-Spandex was Stanley's wife, Audrey Klein-Gray. Earlier that afternoon, she'd neglected to hyphenate. In any case, as soon as table arrangements were settled, Dunn found myself seated next to Hollis, the Unattached.

He learned that the Massachusetts McAllister's were Beacon Hill aristocracy, relatively old Irish money, owners of a chain of hardware stores in the greater Boston area, for which Hollis was general manager. Dunn was thankful she did not want to talk shop, which he found offensive in people who possessed easy money through luck of the draw. She was more willing to ask about his life.

"Nothing to tell, really," Dunn said with a quick smile. He provided an abridged version of a career, sticking to the facts. "Novelist. Divorced. Presently unattached."

This admission earned a smile from Hollis. "Audrey told me all about you."

Dunn could not for the life of him understand how his being unmarried should intrigue a younger woman. In the cruel mathematics of chance, he could have been her father.

"I'm the creator of the Max Sledge Mysteries." He winced at the hope that she might recognize the name.

"Would I know your books? I mean like, are they sold in stores?"

With the wind out of his sails, he listed the names of a novel or two that had achieved a margin in sales. "I'm Ashley Winslow…?" Dunn was tempted but did not explain that his agent and bookbinder agreed that his Christian name was ill suited to a writer of mysteries.

"Not *that* Ashley Winslow!" Hollis shouted in surprise. "I absolutely love his books. You're Ashley Winslow? Omigod, you're Max Sledge," she said, smiling as people do when face to face with previously unrecognized celebrity.

Dunn sheepishly admitted to it. "Well, I *invented* him. I wouldn't say I *am* him."

She insisted on calling him *Max* for the remainder of the evening.

"Which is your favorite?" he asked as the soup was served.

"Favorite?"

"Of my books, which is your favorite?"

Her mainstay of confidence seemed to splinter under the weight of his question.

She offered a brave smile. "Oh," she mewed, "you know the one…where Max is so, I don't know. He was…?"

Saving her, Dunn suggested, "Depressed?" She nodded enthusiastically and sipped wine from her glass, eyeing him over the rim. "*The Prozac Murders.* Where Max discovers his psychotherapist is a serial killer?"

"Yes," she blurted eagerly. "Oh, I *hated* the psychotherapist."

"One of my favorites."

"I knew he did it before, you know, Max Sledge found all those clues…"

Here was the monkey wrench jammed into the machinery of their chitchat. Dunn gave no clues in any of his books because he detested mysteries strewn with hints of evidence to a crime. It was true that this nonconformity had made enemies among adherents to the genre, but as a writer he was meticulously authentic in Max Sledge's criminal investigations, so much so that his books were favorites among police detectives and peace officers across the country.

As he tried to clarify, Hollis changed the subject. "Oh, you know what I mean. Anyway, I simply can't wait for your next one. Are you working on something now?"

Dunn flinched. What was he to say, that she had touched upon his reason for escaping to sea for lack of any fresh ideas? That he had sailed his literary craft into the doldrums?

As an intuitive creature, she read his anxiety and changed the subject. "Tell me something, if you don't mind. What kind of name is *Max*? Is it short for Maximilian or something?"

"Maxfield as in *Maxfield* Parish," answered Dunn.

"Awesome." She smiled warmly and reached out to touch his hand.

They talked authors and novels for hours. Dunn steered her toward his favorites, Raymond Chandler, George Chesbro, Michael Collins, and Elmore Leonard. "I love anything by Elmore Leonard," she said too enthusiastically. Her expression seemed to say that she hoped he wouldn't ask for particulars— Dunn suspected she hadn't read a stitch of Dutch's work. He took great effort to explain that the crime writer's greatest talent was believable dialogue. "Frankly, Dutch and I are friends. We often catch up at PEN conventions." All of it was elaboration, of course, but not pure fabrication. Dunn had met Elmore Leonard once at a book signing—*his*. It is doubtful Mr. Leonard would remember meeting the author of the Max Sledge series.

"Do you really think he's the greatest?" she asked. "Better than say ...oh, you know who I mean...?"

Dunn saved her again by declaring it was a matter of personal preference. He dropped more names of authors he had have never met, "chums with whom I've had the odd cocktail." She was familiar with none of them, to Dunn's relief, and she proposed no further questions, preferring instead to listen politely. Dunn was nothing if not obtuse, showy, and arrogant, anything to distract her from his sweaty palms. Her striking beauty and rapt attention had made a schoolboy of him.

She and Dunn got on famously. As he listened to her explain how long Audrey and she had known one another, Dunn thought about his ex-wife. Marjorie had shown so little interest in his writing career. Two decades of marriage and the most he got was "That's nice, dear." Dunn remembered a particularly ugly morning at the breakfast table when he showed her his short-story nomination for the Pushcart Prize that included a special note from the publisher, commending Dunn's "fine storytelling." What did Marjorie say? *That's nice, dear.* She was so dismissive. But this girl, *this girl* could not stop gushing about the Max Sledge novels. She seemed to know them better than Dunn. She illuminated scenes that the author, for the life of him, could not remember writing. He knocked out four books a year, hastily written in the rough and handed over to the publishing house editor, affording Dunn little time for reflection. He had trouble remembering half the Max Sledge plots.

Dunn questioned her about a car chase that she insisted was in *The Internet Murders*. "Funny you don't recall. And you're the guy who wrote it," she said. "It's just the best. Like something out of *The French Connection*." Dunn assumed that she had confused the movie with his book but he let it go. He didn't want to rock the boat.

Had Dunn not run into Audrey, he would not have been introduced to Hollis. This is pure Kismet, he thought. Destiny had brought them together. And yet, as he sat gazing at her, he knew at the end of the night their conversation would lead to nothing more than a polite handshake or peck on the cheek. Such a lovely girl might agree to hug the famous author to show her admiration but nothing more would happen, surely, no invitation to a private cabin, no romantic strolls on the poop deck. The difference in their ages was a chasm never to be bridged.

As he looked back on it, he could not remember what had been served for dinner that night. He remembered looking so deeply into Hollis's hazel eyes that he thought he might drown. After coffee and Port, the younger people invited Dunn to join them for dancing at an onboard nightclub, but he declined. "I can't say I'd be much fun. Ballroom's more my style, I'm afraid." He thought the young men were relieved to have gotten rid of the old geezer as they shook hands all round. The women kissed the author goodnight on the cheek like the old schoolboy he was. He especially remembered

Hollis McAllister's intoxicating perfume and the feathery feel of her lips on his neck, just below the ear.

Chapter Two

IN DUNN'S SUITE the next day the contrived antique phone jangled. It was Hollis. "How'd you track me down?" Dunn asked. She explained that the Captain's registry had him confused with a guy named Bob Dunn. "When I explained who you were, the one and only *Ashley Winslow*, they connected me. Elementary, my dear Ash," she said. They were on for lunch. She brought two paperbacks for him to autograph.

Dunn asked, "Where'd you get these?" One of the gift shops had a library of supermarket bestsellers, she said. "I thought these were out of print," he reflected. He gave special attention to wording his phrases in the dedication, making them imply more than was immediately apparent. She pressed the books to her bosom like a keepsake.

At lunch, they found an art-gallery theme café near the stern and sat at a small table with a white tablecloth, on two wicker chairs. At another table, a couple was finishing their lunch just as Dunn and Hollis sat down. At that time of day, most of the passengers were standing at the bow, peering through binoculars. An official announcement earlier that morning had alerted passengers to a military vessel ablaze on the horizon. A Russian destroyer or something, it was said, struggled desperately to stay afloat. The Captain had responded to mayday calls in the middle of the night, taking them nearly a hundred nautical miles off course, but by morning two American vessels beat them to the Russian and provided the necessary assistance. The passengers breathed a collective sigh of relief at the good news, but still the majority gawked at the catastrophe and photographed it through expensive telephoto lenses. The near tragedy left Hollis and Dunn to dine without fear of discovery.

At first Hollis acted standoffish, as though in the hour between the telephone call and lunch she had lost all interest in the idea of dining with an old man. But as their conversation progressed, Dunn realized her reticence was nothing more than shyness in the presence of a "famous person," as she called it. He did all that he could to put her at ease. An hour earlier in his suite, Dunn had changed clothes four times, put on three different pairs of shoes, and paraded before the mirror in a hat, which he eventually discarded for the spectacle of a receding hairline. He was nervous as a teenager, but maturity has a way of concealing insecurity behind a web of wrinkles.

Hollis wore a lovely peach cardigan with mother-of-pearl buttons over a simple but provocative dress and a pair of sandals. She looked ripe and edible. She had impeccable taste, in Dunn's opinion. When she complained of a chill, he asked the waiter to move them inside, near the fake fireplace. There she seemed to warm in many ways, and their friendship blossomed, supported in large part by a mutual love of books and a bottle of fine Spanish sherry.

In the beginning, theirs was a father-daughter affair. Dunn did not kid himself that the youthful creature should find him a suitable mate, but he was flattered that she wanted to spend time with him. In their discussion of Vladimir Nabokov's *Lolita*—a one-sided discussion as Hollis confessed her ignorance—Dunn pointed out the differences in their ages, not to draw comparisons necessarily between himself and Humbert Humbert or to make Hollis out as the notorious *nymphet,* but to allude to the obvious. She declared her age abruptly. "I'm close to forty."

Dunn smiled and sipped the amontillado. "I doubt very close." Meaning her age. She said something about the women in her family retaining a youthful appearance well into their fifties. "Well, jolly good for your genetics, my dear," Dunn said. "You look ten years younger, at least. Not a day past thirty."

She seemed offended by the remark. "I'm going to hit the big four-oh next year." And that was the end of that. They said nothing for a time because this discussion of age, a kind of reverse ageism, unnerved Dunn by its disingenuousness. Finally, when he pointed out that the mathematical difference in their ages was the approximate age of his nephew, she threw down her napkin and gave a good performance of being ticked off. She gave him little time to apologize. "What does it matter how old I am or you? Can't we just be friends and forget about this *age thing?*"

He told her that he was willing if she was. "I doubt your friends will see it your way, should we show up arm in arm at dinner with a sheepish countenance."

"I don't know what you mean," she said. "Sheepish what?"

"A lover's countenance."

She shrugged her lovely shoulders.

"Mussed hair, flushed cheeks," Dunn said. "A self-satisfied grin?"

She laughed when she got it, and he discovered that he loved making her laugh. She had a throaty laugh with just a hint of hoarseness that suggested a deep sensuality. When she laughed, her eyes flashed like clear water. Despite himself, he was falling madly in love with her.

⊠   ⊠   ⊠

Halfway across the Atlantic there was a mechanical failure of the water pumps on the mid-decks. The passengers, some of them—Dr. and Mrs. Paulson being the first in line—threatened to sue if hot water was not restored immediately. Dunn was as unsurprised as anyone. He knew the Paulson's for what they were—posers. They had led everyone to believe they belonged in first class. It turned out that they were lodged nowhere near the flying bridge suites of first class. In any event, Dunn had plenty of hot water in his quarters, and none of his neighbors were complaining. "Let the *Doctor* figure it out, that's my attitude," he muttered to himself before the bathroom mirror.

That very afternoon, Dunn received a call from Hollis. "Max, Max? Could I ask a favor?" She needed to impose on him, to use his shower, if indeed the rumors were true that the upper decks had full pressure and hot water. "Of course," he said. He gave his suite number. "I will let you in, and then respectfully, as the gentleman you know me to be, I will take my leave. Give you full advantage of the facilities." She was at his door within the hour with a change of clothes on a hanger.

"Thanks, Max." She went up on her toes to kiss his cheek. "You're such a dear."

She went directly into the bathroom, and Dunn kept to his side of the suite by closing the pocket door separating the bathroom and bedroom from the parlor that looked out on the balcony and sea. He ordered room service, a bottle of Pouilly-Fuissé that he had his eye on but had yet to sample, plus a tray of dates and crackers, bottled water. Once the sound of the shower fell silent, Dunn opened the wine and dried the two crystal wineglasses in a monogrammed towel. Hollis spoke to him through the pocket door. "Max, would you please open this door? It's locked or something."

"Well, I wanted to give you some privacy, young lady. That's all."

Dunn pulled back on the door, and she stood fresh from the shower. She wore a goose-down robe, cuffs rolled back, a shawl collar, hands comfortably at her side, no earrings. Dunn suspected she wore nothing underneath. He stood, gripping the two wine glasses and the Pouilly-Fuissé, feeling utterly foolish. Courage drained away at the sight of her.

Her dark hair was not yet completely dry. She had brushed it back, away from her face, that precious face that Dunn had dreamt about for most of his life. Her eyes were softly engaging and eager at the same time, alluring in the amber light of an afternoon at sea. "What am I to do?" Dunn asked *sotto voce*. "I've fallen in love with you." A gentle smile came to her. She seemed a willing participant in a conspiracy. She came to him and whispered, "And I you."

Three little words changed Dunn's life.

She relieved him of the glasses and wine bottle and placed them on a table. Then, without a word, she reached up, slid her hands behind his neck, and they kissed, she on her bare toes as Dunn fit his hands around the small of her back. Within this Nabokov moment of young girl and old man, they sank into the bed where they began to make love. There were no mutterings about the differences in their ages, his sags contrasting starkly with her taut skin, his hands coarse and loose against her softness.

No declarations of undying love were said in the moment of passion. They were honest with one another. Nothing needed to be said. It was obvious the great chasm of time could not possibly be bridged by sexual intercourse or by their burgeoning love. In the end what they worried about was how to keep the liaison secret from her friends at dinner. As such, Dunn solved the dilemma by gracefully declining to join them.

"I will explain to your friends that I am required to dine with my original seatmates." She gladly accepted his rationalization. "Please, give my regards to Bill and Ned. Sally, et al. And especially Audrey." When they separated for the evening, after kissing passionately at the door to the suite, Dunn ordered dozens of long-stem red roses to be delivered to the staterooms of Hollis, Audrey, Sally, and Bill and Ned, not knowing which of the two men would like roses more than the other. He had the cards signed: *In gratitude for your friendship, Max Sledge.*

His purchases emptied the onboard stores of roses, which cost Dunn a small fortune. Their effect was marvelous. After dinner, all of his new friends bounced over to the first class table where Audrey handled the introductions. The women and Ned gushed and thanked Dunn profusely for the flowers while Mrs. Paulson looked on and nearly cracked a denture, grinding her craw. Mrs. Surmelian believed it was some kind of practical joke and she laughed until she had to excuse herself from table as she had peed her pants. Hollis and Dunn managed not to make too much eye contact, but when they did glance at one another, the electricity leapt the gap. Dunn no sooner returned to his rooms than the phone rang.

"I have to see you, Max," It was Hollis.

"Well, sweetheart," Dunn said, "I'm almost ready for bed."

"That's where I truly want to be. May I come up?"

After making love again, Dunn slept like a log that night, and when he awakened very early he saw Hollis sitting in the chair at his desk. She seemed to be reading something, but often the sleeper misperceives upon waking, pulling away from their dreams. He sat up in bed and rubbed his eyes. He thought to himself that she couldn't be reading his private papers. When she saw that he was awake, she picked up a cup of coffee and said, "Good morning, darling." Dunn realized that he must have been mistaken.

They watched the sunrise off the balcony while eating breakfast in matching bathrobes. Dunn had never known such happiness and sadness mixed together, an ambivalence of high emotion. They both knew that soon—within two short days—they would have to part. She had her itinerary, and Dunn had his. They would go their separate ways, a painful truth they both understood. "Where is your first port of call? After Southampton, I mean?" she asked.

"*Venezia*," Dunn said. "I have rented an apartment in Dorsoduro, a little neighborhood off the beaten path. Away from the tourists. Have you been to Venice?" She shook her head. "You should come. I mean, *go*." He wrote down the telephone number of the apartment and handed her the slip of paper. "If you manage to make your way, be sure to call me. I'll treat you to a marvelous dinner. Is it a deal?"

She was near tears. "Max…would you mind if I came with you? I can't lose you now…so soon."

Dunn stood stock-still. Had he heard her correctly? "What about your friends? What about Audrey? You are traveling together." They will understand, she said. They will just have to. She fell into his arms, and he spoke softly to her. "Of course, you can come with me. But, sweetheart, are you sure? Wouldn't you prefer being with Audrey and Stanley?" She shook her head and repeated that she wanted to be with him. "Okay," he said, pulling away from their embrace to look her in the eye. "If that's what you want, you'll come with me to Venice."

She asked if he was sure in his mind, that this was what he wanted. "I've never been more certain of anything in my whole life," Dunn told her.

For the brief remainder of the crossing, their intimacy had a salutary effect on Dunn's writer's block. The logjam of creativity broke, and his imagination began to fill with fresh ideas, brilliant mysteries and twists of plot. On the last day and night remaining, Dunn pounded out his respectable English on the laptop computer, completing a detailed outline, a twenty-page synopsis and the first couple of chapters. Before the ship docked in Southampton, Dunn emailed his agent and publisher with what he highlighted as "my best Max Sledge Mystery ever!" Hollis had made Bob Dunn/Ashley Winslow/Max Sledge into a new man. Love had transformed the beast of intractable stupidity he had felt for nearly six months, and he was writing again, writing like the reincarnation of Marcel Proust.

✉   ✉   ✉

After disembarking the Northern Star and after a brief good-bye to her friends at Customs, from Southampton they took the train to London. Dunn called his travel agent and arranged for a room at the Langham on Portland Place in the heart of the West End. Here was a five-star hotel to match his enthusiasm for their relationship, which he hoped would continue unimpeded by the difference in their ages.

They arrived by taxi from Paddington Station via the train from Southampton, a little bedraggled and weary. The hotel lights illuminated the façade like the pillars of a commercial bank, dignified and posh. An overnight refuge for celebrities and the rich, the Langham was a prestigious, grand hotel. Dunn and Hollis spent two nights.

At breakfast on their first day in London, she dressed in an Irish sweater and slacks. "Max, if you insist on taking me to expensive hotels, I can't wear *this*," she said. He agreed. They took the morning to shop at Prada on Sloane and Gucci at the Old Bond, for a few essentials that she needed. He spent a small fortune but he had to admit, she looked fantastic in her new clothes, shoes and accessories. To show her off, Dunn bought tickets to the London Symphony Orchestra. In the late afternoon they had aperitifs before heading to the Barbican Centre. They hailed a taxi in the fog and drank champagne in the symphony hall. After Dunn's breathless anticipation that she enjoy herself, Hollis fell asleep before the Choral of Beethoven's Ninth. *"An die Freude...."*

The following morning, after saying good-bye to the Langham, they took a cab to St Pancras Station for the Eurostar to mainland Europe. They rode the *Train à Grande Vitesse* to Paris. He was bleeding cash and credit in his pathetic attempt to impress her. In the dining car, he noticed a few Americans, young men about her age, hanging around and ogling. One of them remarked, "Who's the girl with the old guy?" After she put them in their place with a chilly remark and an inaccessible smile, the tallest of them said, "Why don't you dump grandpa here and come with us? You like to party?" Hollis seemed to be having second thoughts as though the boy had triggered in her a sadness just below the surface. To cheer her up, Dunn ordered the most expensive bottle of champagne on the menu and walked her by the arm past the boys, to their first class compartment. There, he regaled her with promises of gifts and baubles as he poured the champagne.

For three days in Paris in a nice room at the Ritz, all of Dunn's expenses went onto an American Express card. With charges piling up, he felt the need to find an Internet café where he could settle his account online. After locating one, he explained to Hollis, "Darling, I need to take care of some business. You don't mind, do you?" She insisted on accompanying him to the café, despite his assurances that he would not be long. He had hoped she might wish for a little time alone in their room. After hours of shopping in boutiques and lunching at expensive restaurants, Dunn needed the time to sort out her expenditures.

"I want a *patisserie*," she said.

"How do you stay so slim?" he asked. They had just eaten a four-course meal.

In the taxi, she cuddled next to him. "I want something sweet." At the café she fell asleep beside him, her head on his shoulder, the half-eaten pastry left on a plate, as Dunn did his business online.

On their last day in Paris, he persuaded her to forego shopping for a once-in-a-lifetime chance to see "some really cool art." After Dunn had said it, he wished he hadn't. Why hadn't he chosen his words more carefully? *Cool* sounded so Sixties; she seemed to wince at it. "You're in Paris, France, and you want to spend the day at some *art museum?*" she said, registering comic incredulity. Dunn described what they had to look forward to at the Louvre. "Think of the art masterpieces, think of the culture. I thought you liked that sort of thing," he said. In the end, she agreed to go but was not duly impressed, as far as Dunn could tell. Still, she managed to spend some of his money at the Louvre gift shop while ignoring the masterpieces.

Chapter Three

THEY TRAVELED AT NIGHT by train, first class through the Alps, and arrived in Milan the next morning. Dunn rented a Mercedes convertible, and they drove through an early fall rain to Verona, to a small bed and breakfast nestled in the hills.

"How long're we staying here?" she asked.

"Just overnight."

Hollis complained of the pace of their travel. "It's exhausting!" The past few days had been a whirlwind. Why couldn't they stay in Verona, rest up and do a little sightseeing?

"But we have reservations at a palace in Venice, my dear. Verona doesn't hold a candle to the Queen of the Adriatic." He glanced across the front seat of the Mercedes at her, uncertain what to make of this sudden change of mood. She was acting coolly towards him. He believed it had something to do with the boys who had "harassed" her on the train to Paris. He reached across to pat her knee. "You'll see. You'll see," he said, as a father might to a sullen child. She turned away and pouted.

At the Bed & Breakfast, the *padrona di casa* declared theatrically, as Italians so often do, the reservations had been made for one occupant specifically. Not *due personas*, she said with a shake of the finger. After Dunn multiplied the potential bill to twice the amount, she softened and gave them a complimentary bottle of *vino rosso typicale*.

On the following morning after breakfast, they checked out and drove east along the Brenta canal, a postcard of Italy lined by the magnificent houses of the Venetian merchants. Until the day he died, Dunn kept the distinct memory of that morning, the top down on the Benz, racing along the canal road, Hollis raising her bare arms into the Adriatic light and the wind making a riot of her glorious hair. They ate sandwiches at a roadside café, and Dunn leaned across the table to take her hand. "I do love you, you know," he said. She dropped her gaze in an expression that struck him as something close to embarrassment or shame.

In Venezia, Antonella met them at the Hertz office with her doddering black lab. She was a pleasant, intelligent woman whose abilities contrasted sharply with the old crone from the Verona B&B. She and Dunn could have been great friends in another life. Antonella was a divorced mother of a mature daughter. Her occupation was as architectural restorer, a suitable profession for a Venetian. More than once, Antonella made the mistake of referring to Hollis as Dunn's daughter. She—Hollis—rolled her eyes at the gaff, but he made no effort to correct the landlady. What did it matter what she thought? If it pleased the landlady to think of them as traveling father and daughter, so be it. Hollis was not so forgiving, as she was displeased by the assumption. She sighed like a child at each of Antonella's singsong referrals to *"belissima* daughter." To appease her, Dunn squeezed her hand and accompanied this with a mocking scowl. "Let it go," he whispered.

Antonella spent an hour, first guiding them through the maze to her majestic house, and later by introducing them to the particulars of the kitchen, bathroom and living room. Left on their own to unpack, Hollis went from room to room rearranging things and speaking at the top of her voice about how offensive the landlady was. Why did Max not speak up in her defense? What does "that old hag" (she was a shade younger than Dunn) think she is implying? Her anger seemed to rise with each complaint that she voiced in a high register. He did the best he could to give the storm of her emotions free rein; perhaps the gale would blow itself out.

Dunn retreated to the large main room. He opened the windows and doors leading to a small balcony to admit the cool fresh sea air. Church bells rang out from every quarter of the city. But along with this, mosquitoes came too, torturing him. In a chair as he read from a book by Goethe, he imagined himself from the viewpoint of biting insects, a blubbering mass full of hot delicious blood. Hollis shut herself in the bedroom.

In the evening, Dunn opened a bottle of wine and brought Hollis a glass as a peace offering. He said that she should learn to pick and choose her battles. "It wasn't one worth fighting, Hollis, believe me." She continued to pout, and there was no matter of persuasion on Dunn's part that would assuage her. Eventually, she fell asleep on the couch in the main room while Dunn opened his laptop to check in with publisher and agent over his latest book proposal.

He learned from his agent that the bookseller had expressed profound doubt about publishing another Max Sledge Mystery, considering his last two attempts had not recouped publishing costs. Not merely a new twist of plot in the series was requested but "something completely new." They were no longer interested, as the publisher put it, "in beating a dead horse." Ashley Winslow was too passé for the publisher's new audience, the youthful demographics of today's readers poorly matched to so archaic a genre.

His new editor, assigned to him after the unexpected demise of Gary Feikenbaum, God rest his brilliant soul, was flexing her adolescent muscle. She was playing the role of gifted editor, which had yet to be proven, by taking hypothetical scissors to his ideas and snipping them to bits. Furious, Dunn wrote a nasty note to Glenda, his agent, that he was not happy, *not in the least*, with this new editor. "I am of half a mind to sue myself out of contract," he wrote, "and go with another house, notwithstanding our years of success there." Then he fired off an ugly message to the editor. Dunn told Ms. Felicity Jane that he was in no mood for major changes to his latest Max Sledge proposal. He said that it was a passably good idea in its present form, in his humble opinion, and that while on vacation in Europe he would have the time to deliver a completed manuscript in less than a month. She, the editor, would just have to be patient for the muse to work her magic.

This, of course, was a lie. Hollis was taking up more of his time to write as they crossed Europe. And in this tender stage of their relationship, he wanted to be attentive to her needs, as immature and irrationally demanding as she was. Despite this change of circumstance in his personal life, Dunn was not about to be pushed around by a snot-nosed MFA graduate from Bryn Mawr with a literary twitch up her ass. As he sent email after email, he imagined the conference calls and meetings that Ms. Felicity Jane would take with his agent, sipping her soy latte and barking commands like Lord and Commander, for God's sake. Dunn could imagine her ordering underlings, men twice her age, to pick up her dry cleaning; telling executive assistants to get Richard Ford or Jay McInerney on the line to discuss their latest manuscripts; or get someone to tell Cormac his interview with *The New York Times Book Review* was on no matter what, come hell or high water, etc. Over the years of slaving away at the keyboard, pounding out the Max Sledge series, Dunn was responsible for a bright pile of cash for his publisher, certainly not in the league of Nick Burns or Jay Pederson, but at least a million dollars, perhaps more. And what about his loyal fans, what would the bookseller say to them after canceling his successful series of mysteries? Who in hell did Ms. Felicity Jane think she was dealing with, some kind of amateur?

He shut down the laptop when he heard Hollis stir. He found her in a much-improved mood, thankfully. They went out for a romantic candlelight dinner along the canals, *al fresco* despite the threat of rain. Rain was in the forecast for the following morning as well, and it made good. Piazza San Marco flooded from high tides and runoff. The flood kept them indoors and out of danger. They lounged, read, made love, ate a rudimentary lunch in their little kitchenette, opened a bottle of Chianti, drank half of it, made love again and napped until the late afternoon. Dunn did everything but write. In the evening, beneath a splendid golden sunset, they strolled the slick cobbles of Venice. Hollis wore one of her new dresses that they'd purchased in London, and Dunn looked dapper in his Hamburg hat and off the shoulder cape. Hollis said the outfit, which at first he had refused to wear, made him look the distinguished literati. They went back to their apartment and made love again. As Dunn was falling asleep he realized, by counting the number of times on his hand, that he had made love to this young woman more times that week than he had in the last five years. Needless to say, he slept with a smile on his face.

⊠　　⊠　　⊠

Dunn read a quote from the book he'd brought along on his trip to Europe. In it Goethe had called Venice "Bride of the Sea," which he thought a lovely sentiment.

Their neighborhood in Dorsoduro had a block of university student housing. Otherwise, it was home to working class folks and their children who played soccer on the ancient flagstones. The campo S. Margherita with its market and assorted shops provided for their needs, except for fine pastries. These they bought elsewhere. Dunn found a barge near Ponet al Pugni that sold produce, and at Margaret du Champ, Hollis shopped for wine and the makings for lunch and dinner. Upon their return to the *palazzo*, they stopped to watch artists hard at work on stools, their brushes and pens flying across sheets of paper. Hollis remarked that the light was pinkish gold in the morning, and purple-gold at evening. "It is so quiet," she said. No automobiles, Dunn assured her with a smile. No cars, only the soft voices of Italians as they walked along the calle to their jobs.

They conducted a "museum crawl," as Hollis called it, to admire Tintoretto's at the S. Georgio Cathedral where they climbed the steps to a bell tower for a full view of all the islands of Venice. In the cathedral, Dunn paid for and lit a candle for his friend back in the States who'd been given a terminal medical diagnosis. Hollis lit one as well, but she would not say for whom. Dunn remarked, "I should have ignited a middle-aged birthday cake full of candles." He meant, for how worried he was for his friend.

Over the passage of days and nights, Dunn found himself drinking too much wine and espresso. After Hollis bought a pack of Muratti's, he took up cigarette smoking in the evening to accompany the *vino rosso*. "Italy is a sexy country," he said to Hollis. "But it's probably going to kill me."

After a week of routine, of shopping in the mornings for lunch and dinner at Campo Santa Margarita (Dunn was elected chef for their everyday meals), of exploring and touring museums, the Piazza and San Marco cathedral, the Doges, Hollis grew bored by it all. At dinner one night over a lovely salmon steak, Dunn suggested that they consider a change of venue. "Would a Greek isle suit you?" At first she thought he must be joking, but when he pulled out tickets for passage on a ferry to Greece, she was her old self again. She was on the phone to her friends, who had ended up somewhere in Amsterdam. She bragged to them about their palace in Venice and where they were headed next. Dunn remembered her specifically giving the name of the hotel on the Greek island where they held reservations.

And so the new lovers bid farewell to the apartment and Antonella as they made their way aboard the ferry Ikarus to the Greek Isle of Corfu, to a little fishing village of chalky houses with terracotta roofs, bright blue and crimson boats resting on the strand, nets and squid drying in the harsh sunlight. After two nights in the hotel, they rented a small apartment on a high hill overlooking the Adriatic— *As wine-dark as the Aegean*, Dunn mused.

They were happy for a short time until once again Hollis seemed to drift unconsciously into melancholy. Of course, Dunn considered his advanced age as the cause. He was too old for her, that old refrain. He began to accept that she would have preferred younger men, boys with whom she had more in common. But when he broached the subject of her gloominess, he did so without being direct. He nibbled around the edges of his presumption before coming right out with it. "It's because I'm old, isn't it?" She assured him that she was perfectly happy with him; that it was her "period," and that she was always like this a few days beforehand. Here was something Dunn knew very little about. He didn't know if the few women he dated on rare occasions even menstruated. But he did wonder how it was possible to be moody now in addition to one week earlier in Venice, a mood that was the impetus to relocate to a Greek isle. Did she have two cycles in one month? No, he concluded, she was lying. But why would she lie? He fell back on his old standby for an excuse that he was, indeed, too old for her.

Not being familiar with the fairer sex, Dunn had heard it said that women at times of hormonal imbalance will go on a shopping spree, and this was where he took Hollis. They took the ferry to Brindisi where they spent the day shopping for new Italian shoes for her. They visited an international bank, and there Dunn showed Hollis how he used his credit card to transfer funds to his "vacation account," as he called it. He showed her twice because the first time she said she was absolutely clueless about "high finance." She seemed eager to learn such things for her future, to build up a portfolio for her retirement, she explained. Laden with five pairs of shoes in boxes, they stopped at a camera store when an expensive Canon Digital caught her eye. Dunn bought it for her. She took many pictures during the crossing, mostly of Dunn at the rail holding a glass of Greek beer and secretly deploring the fact that he had yet to write another paragraph of the new novel.

One day, at the beach, as Dunn sat in umbrella shade to protect his skin, Hollis lay sprawled on a chaise lounge beneath the brilliant Greek sun. While she got a tan, he was busy writing postcards to friends back home, to his literary agent, his lawyer and investment adviser, and to the President of the Vacaville Women's Literary League.

"It's spelled with a 'K' you know."

Dunn looked behind. Hollis was reading over his shoulder. "Didn't know you'd gotten up."

She continued to read and ignore him.

"What's spelled with a 'K'?" he asked.

"*Korfu.*" She snapped her finger against the postcard. "It's not spelled with a 'C'."

Then she lay back down on the chaise, arching toward the sky in her Jackie Kennedy sunglasses and ignoring him. Dunn looked in amazement at this seductive creature who had fallen into such a state of malcontent. Shaking his head in disbelief, he returned to his stack of postcards. He tried to remember how long she had been like this. A week, ten days? And now she had taken up the dishonest practice of sneaking up on him to read private letters. He had to admit, more than a few of her personality traits struck him as bipolar. Up one minute and down the next. Happy today, a miserably dour bitch the next. Very early on in their relationship, Dunn had gained the wisdom and given up trying to interpret her moods. From then on he went with the flow.

His prayers for a change in her mood had gone unanswered. She still argued with him over petty nonsense, and even now, at the beach, they weren't on speaking terms, not really. Not as they had been on the Northern Star.

Dunn looked up at the warm, peaceful scene of fishing boats resting on a perfect sea. He noticed a pack of young people, around Hollis's age, frolicking half naked on the strand. The boys wore the skimpiest of thongs and the girls were topless. After assessing them from behind her sunglasses, Hollis asked, "Do you find them attractive?"

How does one reply to such a question? Dunn told her, "Yes, I suppose, if you mean the attraction men feel for all women who expose their breasts, but no…" She clicked her tongue when he assured her, "They don't hold a candle to you."

She turned away, toward the rollicking young people.

He was taken by surprise when she removed her top in an impetuous fling of the hand. She did so with such speed, Dunn had little time to react. As she settled back on the chaise, he almost picked up his towel to wrap around her shoulders but he considered her present mood and had second thoughts.

After a few minutes, one of the boys in a black thong, skin parched brown, sauntered over to them. Hollis was on her back, arms overhead, relaxed, her breasts exposed, while this impudent rascal smirked and gazed down upon the beauty. In halting English he asked if Hollis would make him "the luckiest man on world" and agree to join his friends for a drink at the bar. Dunn could tell that she was intrigued by the invitation. She looked to Dunn for approval, and he fell easily into the role of father figure. "If it will make you happy," he said with a shrug. She made up her mind in an instant and repaired the top of her bathing suit to its proper place. She retrieved her straw handbag and kissed him on the cheek. "I won't be long," was all she said.

By ten o'clock that night, Dunn knew it was over. He packed his bags and made the necessary arrangements for a ferry ride back to Venice. When Hollis did finally manage to return the following morning, she looked the worse for wear but pleased with herself. She gestured at his suitcases tucked neatly against the wall in the entry. He was dressed in his traveling duds. He was smoking a cigarette, the first of many that day, and drinking a glass of Uzo, the hour be damned. He melodramatically stubbed out the smoke and joined her at the door.

They didn't have to say much to one another. She knew, he knew. Dunn tried to assure her when she showed tears that he was not upset in the least. It was a lie, but a necessary one. When he insisted that she keep the gifts, the dresses, shoes, and camera, it seemed to please her. She seemed put off that he had paid for an extra week at the apartment so she could enjoy herself with her new friends. She acted as though plans had already been hatched and they did not include staying in Corfu.

"I knew this couldn't last," Dunn said, holding her close for the last time. "It wasn't meant to be, my darling." It was a line stolen from the fictional mind of Ashley Winslow and put into the mouth of Max Sledge. He kissed her forehead, picked up the bags and walked to the waiting taxi.

Chapter Four

ON THE CROSSING to Venice, Dunn made plans to resume his Grand Tour that had been so beautifully interrupted by Hollis. If memory served, he should have been in Amsterdam by now. Onboard he sat at the bar, nursing the last of a second beer, and drawing lines in red pencil on a EuroRail Map. He planned to take a train from Venice to Milan and, from there, an even slower train to Amsterdam via Metz, France, where he would transfer in the middle of the night. He lifted the pencil from the map. There was something about the Netherlands as a destination that sparked a memory.

At the ticket kiosk in Venice, he remembered Hollis had mentioned something about her friends having "landed in the Netherlands." The risk of bumping into them almost persuaded Dunn to change his itinerary, but he reconsidered. The chances of his running into Audrey and Stanley were nil as far as he could see. Amsterdam was a big city. Plenty of room for expatriated Americans to get lost in. He had no interest in staying for an extended period in the Netherlands. He had targeted it as a destination for the art museums, but only for one or two nights. In the original itinerary, it had been intended as a stopgap on his way to Copenhagen.

"The Netherlands," Dunn said to himself. The word *nether* means hindmost or posterior. Dunn was at a loss as to why the historical Dutch would have named their country after something that comes last. Nevertheless, he was on his way to another city of canals.

In Europe, travel by rail is preferable to the automobile especially if accompanied by a broken heart. European trains are marvelous contraptions full of pleasant amenities, smoking cars and surprisingly good food. They run on time, by and large, and are comfortable if one springs for first class rather than coach. In Venice, Dunn hired a compartment to himself, using up about half of the ready cash he had in his billfold, confident upon arrival that he could draw more from an ATM. He slept a good part of the way beneath a blanket in his clothes, a hardcover of *Death in Venice* by Thomas Mann lolling in his lap. He managed to read half of it before giving up, and from his suitcase of books, selecting Kafka. His feelings of alienation and torment were well matched.

On his second night away from Hollis, he briefly got off to stretch his legs when the train stopped in the Alps. Snow flurries swirled in the lights of the station. Hawkers, bundled in woolen caps and coats, sold sandwiches and iced beer. He shunned these for something warmer and more appetizing, later in the club car. Once, after a change of trains in Metz, three French teenagers forced their way into his compartment at an ungodly hour. Dunn called for security, and the conductor efficiently disposed of them for not having identification or valid tickets. Alone again, he fell into the doldrums of reading, nodding off, and occasionally making his way to the couplings between cars for a smoke or to the bar for a shot of something strong. This was how Bob Dunn's passage to Amsterdam proceeded.

The city is a festival. This was what he thought of Amsterdam as he first saw it through the windows of the club car. Triple-arched bridges strung in Christmas lights over black canals that slid between apartment blocks and side streets. Anne Frank had tried to hide here from the Nazi terror. It was where Rembrandt painted until he went blind. Where Van Gogh lost his mind, and where Vermeer let the light sift through his transparent oils.

Dunn hoped that Amsterdam might restore his sense of adventure so that he could finish his European tour, if not optimistically then at least with a renewed enthusiasm for the spirit of travel. Perhaps the multinational feel of the city would spark the writer in him and he could return again to his latest novel. The manuscript that he carried within the storage disc of his laptop, although weightless, had taken on the heavy burden of guilt for languishing as an incomplete idea. He knew that his livelihood depended upon delivering a spectacularly crafted Max Sledge Mystery, if he were ever to hope to continue the series and recoup the financial cost of his foolishness with Hollis McAllister.

As the train arrived at the Centraal rail station and he made his way through the crowds, a lady approached to ask, "Are you looking for a room? If so, you are welcome to stay at my place. With breakfast, yes?" So as not to get swooped up in the arms of this lady, Dunn thanked her. "I already have a place to stay," he said with a smile, burdened as he was by luggage and his computer bag.

Before heading to his hotel, one recommended and booked at a tourist information center in Metz, he stopped at a marijuana bar a few blocks from the train station. He did so out of innocent curiosity. He was hungry, and the colorful pictures of food in the window caught his eye. With his belongings strewn around him, seated at a corner table, he ate a plateful of sliced sausages and marvelous cheeses. He mused at the stoned habitués of the place. There were the occasional hippies and dead-enders, mostly males with long stringy hair, patchy beards, and hollowed eyes; people that you would have imagined laid about a marijuana bar. But Dunn was surprised to see legitimate business people, men and women smartly dressed, speaking politely to one another, smoking joints and drinking espresso.

When a comely young woman approached his table, looking like a nightclub moll straight out of a Max Sledge novel, he asked about the prices for the marijuana cigarettes arrayed on her serving dish. She explained that costs ranged from cheap to expensive, left to right, depending upon the strength of the herb. The smaller joints on the far right, she said, had a "powerful punch." Not for the weak of heart, she cautioned. Despite his decline, she insisted that he take a sample. "For free," she assured him. When he said that he had no matches, hoping this would be the end of it, she presented an elaborate torch and flicked it to flame. Dunn had no choice but to smoke the thing.

He'd never been stoned before, and so he did not know what to expect. The first clue that something odd was happening were the figures he worked with on a napkin, doing his best to calculate how much he'd spent on Hollis McAllister, all for naught. A few nights at one of the most expensive hotels in London, the digital camera, an entirely new wardrobe and the endless pairs of shoes. No matter how many times he added up the column of numbers, the sums were different. *Nonsense*, he thought. Arithmetic had always been child's play for him. In his effort to focus, further amusements distracted him—a lilting Bach concerto coming from two impossibly small speakers over the front door; the exquisitely frothy taste of his cappuccino; how a girl's cleavage at an adjacent table caught the autumn sunlight. He forgot all about the columns of figures, and for the moment, his troubles seemed remote and attenuated.

The pleasant effect of the marijuana turned to jaw-grinding shock when the waitress returned to the table with his bill and credit card. Although they had some language difficulties—he spoke Tour-Book phrases and she a guttural version of Dutch lingo—

it was clear that the bank had rejected his card. She tossed it on the table, and said something in French that sounded like, "This will not do!"

Nonplused, he retrieved the credit card and presented another. He had half a dozen in his wallet, colorful rectangles from a variety of banks with pictures of himself as a much younger man. He made the point of displaying them as proof of his substantiality, a financial bulwark in plastic if you will. But when each card was rejected, fear gripped Bob Dunn, writer of mysteries. How was this possible? Was the bank's confusion over the credit card merely a factor of his getting high on weed? Paranoia gripped him. Had something happened to America, something that had completely escaped his notice while he lounged in the arms of Hollis McAllister? He realized, he hadn't watched the news on television or read an *International Herald Tribune* for weeks. Had another crisis like 9/11 caused a market crash or the financial markets to close? Anything could have happened. He paid cash for the meal and the marijuana cigarette, which he discovered had not been complimentary after all. Humiliated by the misunderstanding, he gathered up his things and made his way to the hotel, shaken but not defeated.

Although the desk receptionist was an understanding soul, patient and kind, the rejection that Dunn faced in the restaurant proved the same at the hotel. None of his credit cards was accepted, and he offered to pay cash. The receptionist asked if he were ill. "No, why do you ask?" he said. Your eyes, she replied, they are so red. The concierge was considerate enough to store his luggage until a room became available—Dunn kept the laptop because it contained personal information—while he went in search of a bank to resolve this dilemma. However, he received no satisfaction at the bank.

His "vacation account" had been emptied of assets, zeroed out two days earlier. An imposter using his name, account number and passcode from an unknown European location had made the withdrawal. "But I haven't made any withdrawals," Dunn told the bank vice president. "If I had, I wouldn't be here to draw out more of my money." The vice president extended his sincerest sympathies but there was nothing he could do. To prove his point, he pushed copies of the withdrawal printouts across the desk and tapped the row of five zeros proceeded by the symbol for the euro dollar. Dunn had not been cleaned out completely. To his relief, his primary savings account—the principal investment meant to last for the years of his retirement—was intact. But how safe was the nest egg? Someone had his passcode.

He stumbled out of the bank for a bench beside a canal, beneath a tall beech tree. There he sat dejectedly, in complete disregard for the pigeon droppings that spackled the bench. *What has the world come to?*—he asked himself. It didn't take a genius to figure out what had happened. It took only half an hour of recovering from a marijuana high to connect the dots to Hollis McAllister and her friends. What else was he to think? His mind kept ranging back to her cozying up beside him at the bank in Brindisi. She had expressed such a keen interest in the "high finance" of withdrawal of funds and the use of Internet banking connections. Of course, it took accessing his bank accounts twice in her presence—*I am such a fool!*—to give her enough time to memorize the numbers and passcodes.

From the bench by the canal, he retreated to a coffee bar to collect his thoughts and to assess the damage. The small café had WiFi capability. He opened his laptop and notified the banks to cancel his credit card accounts. His emails sounded like fire alarms, "My identity has been stolen along with my account number." After studying the disclaimers at the websites, he summed up the liability limits that he held on each card. The fiasco would cost him tens of thousands of dollars. All of his accounts were maxed out. One card had been used for a down payment on an Alfa Romeo in Athens. He had no doubt whose hands were on the wheel of that fine automobile.

Next, he contacted his broker and explained the situation, asking her to transfer a few thousand dollars from his retirement savings into a new account. Almost instantly, a reply popped up on screen that the passcode on his account had been changed and that the brokerage was unable to abide by the request. To do so, he would need to make the changes in person at a branch office in New York City. Dunn accessed the website and tried to change the passcode on his vacation account. For some reason, an error message popped up on screen each time he hit the Enter button. Essentially, he was locked out of the account for the time being.

Then Dunn fired off emails to friends in the States, his agent and lawyer. It is truly a global society when a writer of mediocre mysteries, sitting in a small café in Amsterdam, can send instant messages to a New York literary agency and his San Francisco tax attorney's office. Because of the nine-hour time difference, however, replies were not forthcoming. He would have to wait another three hours for New York and five to six hours for Bill Martin in San Francisco to check his email.

In the meantime, he decided to do a little detective work on his own. He Googled "McAllister/Boston" and toggled through the first dozen of eight thousand hits. At first flush, there were no hardware stores owned by the Boston McAllister's. Also, no one named McAllister lived on Beacon Hill, a statistical anomaly in itself. When he narrowed his search by typing in "Audrey Gray" he learned that the Internal Revenue Service had liens on all property owned and future income earned by someone named Ms. A. L. Rowland, AKA "Audrey Gray," a former inmate of the Indiana women's penal system. Mining the data became frustrating when he typed the name Stanley Gray, which didn't cough up much of anything.

He switched from the general databases in the search engine to the Cunard Cruise Line shipping registry. He scrolled down the passenger manifest for the Northern Star and found his own name. "I'm getting somewhere," he told himself. Dr. (Walter) and Mrs. Paulson, the Seabrook's, and even the ancient Mrs. Surmelian were on the list, first name Eudora. But no Hollis McAllister. No Mr. and Mrs. Stanley Gray. How was it possible for three people to take a cruise on the prestigious passenger liner and not show up in the manifest? If they had used aliases, how could they have been so cavalier about it? They must have known that a Cunard employee could have called them by a false name at any time, thus blowing their cover. Perhaps they had boarded using disguises, forfeiting their passports to one purser only to retrieve them from another? He thought, *Wasn't that the plot in my* Golden Sunset Mystery? Perhaps they had a friend, an insider, who worked for Cunard? No matter how they pulled it off, Dunn had to accept the fact that they must have planned the heist for over several months time, working out details. They had invested their own resources with confidence, knowing they could execute the caper without a hitch.

"Why me?" he wondered aloud.

It became clear to Dunn. A "famous" writer of successful novels—scores of them—shows up on a ship's manifest. He reserves a suite, which implies that the novelist is extremely wealthy, contrary to reality. They probably researched and discovered his marital status. Here again, his tepid fame had placed him in harm's way. This time the only side benefit of his notoriety was that he got to sleep with a much younger woman. But the pleasures were short-lived. His paramour had ripped him off for a significant amount of money.

He looked up and saw his reflection in the café mirror. The face of a tired old patsy looked back. Bob Dunn, AKA Ashley Winslow, the mark. The luckless fool. Audrey, Stanley and Hollis had recognized a pigeon when they saw one, and they had gone to a great deal of effort to steal him blind.

How could I have been so stupid?

He searched the ocean liner manifest again, this time using first names only. He came up with the names Audrey Lyn Rowland, Stanley Bledsoe and Holister Ehrlich. Hollis, going by Holister, could have misrepresented herself as male, then once onboard, she could have discarded the disguise and gone by Hollis McAllister. All of it was beginning to confuse Dunn, the change of names, the loss of thousands of dollars, all of his troubles mixed up together with a wizened marijuana hangover. The pit of his stomach was sick with worry.

The realization that he had been seduced not by a beautiful young woman but by his own vanity began to sink in. To think that the likes of Hollis McAllister—or whatever she called herself—would take to the bed of a washed-up geezer without an ulterior motive was the height of hubris. Blind arrogance had done away with the likes of Oedipus and Lear. Dunn supposed, at least he was in good company. "I must have been blind," he muttered to himself. "How could I have expected…such an *old fool.*" An old woman in a faded print dress and seated at an adjacent table looked up and scowled, having overheard his comment. Dunn managed to smile but not convincingly. The old woman grappled with a cane and pushed out of her chair, mumbling what must have been a derogatory phrase as she relocated to another table.

Keep your thoughts to yourself, Dunn. He stared at the glowing screen of the laptop, at the pulsing cursor. Now is not the time for pointless regrets, he was thinking. Now is time for the elderly to take revenge on the young.

He resolved not to let the snot-nosed buggers get away with it. He had his pride, after all, not to mention the tens of thousands in stolen vacation dollars to consider.

But what was he to do? He was penniless in a foreign country, in Europe (!) where a flat broke American would not last long. He had three hundred and thirty-seven euros in his billfold, enough to get by for a few days. With the credit cards rendered as nothing but useless plastic and his vacation account cleaned out, he would be forced to rely on the generosity of friends from across the Atlantic. He hoped Glenda could afford a few hundred. He knew Martin was good for it. He wondered if the publisher would pony up an advance to see him through this mess. In spite of the impediment of Ms. Felicity Jane's revisionism, his latest Max Sledge novel promised to take in a modest profit, if he ever managed to finish it.

Dunn resolved to sit tight and be patient. His friends would come through; he had no doubt. He was not without outside resources. His credit was still good, irrespective of the current situation, which should be resolved in a day or two. In the meantime, he would beg Glenda to wire a few hundred to the hotel and ask the publisher for a hefty advance for a plane ticket home. Perhaps Bill Martin could part with some of the money Dunn had been paying him over the years to watch the nest egg, now that Hollis was trying to steal it.

The laptop beeped. It was his agent, Glenda. "What is this about being destitute, another of your ploys prior to our contract negotiations later this year? LOL," she wrote. He sent an Instant Message in reply. *No, no joke. Wallet stolen. Credit cards useless. I'm cleaned out. Send cash.* He provided her with the name and phone number of his hotel in Amsterdam. She was a darling. Very sympathetic. Dunn could almost hear the sincere cries of empathy through the WiFi. "Would fifteen hundred be enough? You'll receive a cashier's check as soon as I can get it to you," she wrote. "Have you contacted the police?"

And then it struck him: what in hell was he doing sitting in an espresso bar when what he should be doing was contacting the police? He thanked Glenda in shorthand and begged off. *Have tons to do. Arrangements to make for flight home, etc. I must go. Thanks again. Love, Bobby.* He then asked the barrister for the location of the nearest police station and quickly made his way there through the maze of Amsterdam.

Chapter Five

WHERE DID YOU LAST use your credit cards, Monsieur?" the Interpol inspector asked.

By the end of the day, Dunn had been through the ringer. He was scarcely able to repeat his name for the umpteenth time in retelling the story to one police officer after another. He had visited two Amsterdam police stations, a local and the downtown headquarters, before being directed to the office of Interpol.

"Your problem is an issue *internationale*," the chief of police had informed him.

"How is this an international issue? I thought the EU had done away with border restrictions and the rest of it," Dunn had said. The Chief expressed his sincerest regrets in the case of the writer's bad luck but his hands were tied. He was, after all, an American citizen visiting a foreign country. Therefore, the "issue *internationale*."

Ergo, he sought the help of Interpol.

"I repeat, Monsieur, when did you last use your credit cards?"

"In Greece, I think."

The Interpol inspector resembled a minor character from a Max Sledge novel, a corrupt Chicago police lieutenant. At the book's end, he had killed him off but not without serious repercussions from rabid fans. Some readers loved Lieutenant Murkowski. Others loved to hate him. All lamented his "death." Couldn't the author bring him back? Why not resurrect him for a later installment? One of the more inventive readers recommended that the writer "do" a series of retrospectives, novels taking place at a time before the death of Lieutenant Murkowski. "Like the *Stars Wars* movies," the reader had proposed. Never having seen *Star Wars*, Bob Dunn did not know what to make of the suggestion.

That aside, Inspector Emile Valadon looked like a dead character out of a mystery novel. His skin was the color and texture of bleached vellum. Over this pasty canvas were two half-lidded eyes and insipid purple lips more suitable to a Super Model than a criminal investigator. Valadon's inflection and demeanor matched his physical appearance: haughty disinterest refined to the height of Chauvinism. He was the quintessential Frenchman who spoke English in a thick accent. Dunn's French was sketchy. The writer had graduated from the Mime School of Foreign Languages. Nevertheless, they muddled through. Quite the odd couple. As long as Dunn played the role of unwashed heathen to his supercilious pre-eminence, they got along well enough.

Inspector Valadon was in Amsterdam on a brief rotation from Lyons, the permanent administrative headquarters of the International Criminal Police Organization or Interpol. Hence, his nationality and brief exile. Leave it to say, the French have a peculiar view of the world, not unlike New Yorkers' view of the rest of America, of anything west of the Hudson River. Aside from Frank Culture there is, according to the French, nothing worth discussing; nothing compares favorably to French cuisine and wine; for fine art there is Musée du Louvre, against which other museums pale. Let the American Press call them "cheese eating surrender monkeys," the French are, at least in their own minds, the foundation of civilization and the only *cause célèbre* for its continuance. Inspector Valadon did not disappoint this stereotype, but rather enlarged upon it.

Valadon asked questions, and when Dunn supplied answers, the inspector jotted them down in a notebook at his desk inside the offices at Interpol. At the beginning of their interview, he had offered a cup of coffee. His assistant, a skinny young man with a painful-looking Adam's apple, fetched two espressos. The coffee was horrible. Dunn left his largely untouched; Inspector Valadon tossed his back in a single swig, eyes watery from the bitterness. "Zee Dutch and their coffee, eh?" That was all he had to say on the matter. With social amenities out of the way, they spent the remainder of the hour going over details of the crime, the names of Hollis McAllister and the Gray's, names that Dunn cautioned were probably aliases. He provided his email address along with the address to his hotel in town, where he hoped to spend the night. "Do you…does Interpol, have a high success rate in these cases?" Dunn asked. "You know, of retrieving my money?"

"Do not concern yourself, Monsieur," the inspector said, clicking his pen and slapping shut the casebook. "In such cases, we always, as you Americans say, *get zee man*, eh?" He laughed, but Dunn did not join him. A feeling of despair over his untenable position descended with its full weight of horror and helplessness.

After he ushered the writer out the door with guarantees and assurances that "all will be well in zee end," Dunn stood at the curb of the busy street, uncertain where to turn or who to lean on for support. He had never, not since the middle of his divorce, felt so awfully alone.

He stood in front of the police station and wondered which way to go. A man who walked two dogs on a lead and appeared intoxicated, offered to give him a helping hand. Dunn had his doubts at first, but by the time the drunk led him to a taxi stand, he was glad to have trusted him. He feared the drunk had been leading him to a mugging. He returned to the hotel where the desk clerk and bellhops eyed him suspiciously as he retrieved his luggage from the concierge and lumbered upstairs to his room where he would wait for Credit Suisse to receive and process a check from Glenda, his literary agent.

On the following day, Dunn hailed a cab and visited a museum to see paintings by Rembrandt, Vermeer, Franz Hals, and a myriad of Dutch painters. Standing alone before a painting by Van Gogh—his last painting of a cornfield with black crows, like pestilence, flying low against a wicked sky, and three existential ruts running divergently through the field—Dunn contemplated the artist's idea of desperation. Van Gogh had shot himself in just such a field, or at least an actor depicting the artist had done so in a movie. Dunn recalled the film. Montgomery Cliff had played Gauguin, and Kirk Douglas played Van Gogh. Dunn turned to a more optimistic painting because he found his mood descending into despair over his own situation.

Outside the museum, from a nearby chocolate factory, the air smelled like a fine candy bar. On his way back to the hotel, he took the chance of boarding an electric train that he hoped would take him east. He'd chosen well. The train had saved him precious euros. That night, he went out to dinner at an Indonesian restaurant and ordered a variety of foods he was unfamiliar with—fried bananas, honey-coated fruit, purple rice with chunks of candied pineapple, chicken fried in peanut oil, and sautéed squash flowers. For around twenty euros, he ate well from about fifteen small plates. In his hotel room, sitting on the bed, he laid out all of his bills and coins and counted how much he had left. He would have to conserve more carefully, he decided, before Glenda's check was scheduled to arrive. He could afford one more night at the hotel, but after that…well, after that he was at a complete loss as to what to do.

He could name the moment his desperation worsened to complete despair. It was the following day when a bank officer at ING turned to him and said, "There's something wrong with your passport, sir."

Dunn had gone to cash Glenda's cashier's check, having now spent his last remaining euros to pay for the hotel room. He was not worried, not after the desk clerk had delivered the good news earlier that morning: the funds had arrived overnight via FedX. The check was as good as cash. But at the bank he'd grown impatient when the teller and an officer, a woman with snow-white hair, spoke privately while making the occasional gesture at the check and in Dunn's general direction. Soon his confidence vanished and was replaced by a rising uneasiness. He asked the teller for the return of his passport and cashier's check, but his request was ignored. He asked again, in an impatient voice. "Please, sir, be patient!" the mature bank officer demanded. When he began pounding on the Plexiglas and insisting on the return of his passport, two security guards manhandled him. He refused to cooperate, not being too familiar, even then, with the guttural caterwauling of the Dutch, and they wrestled him to the floor, cinched his wrists with plastic handcuffs, and locked him in a windowless room. Soon, the police arrived in crisp forget-me-not blue uniforms with yellow scrambled eggs for applets, two boys half Dunn's age. He was transported in the back of a petite white police van to the local police station, with which he was regrettably familiar, and from there to Interpol where he found himself in the afternoon once again facing Inspector Valadon.

"So," the inspector mused, elbows on the desk, chin in his hands, "what are we to do with you, Monsieur?"

Inspector Valadon was in possession of Dunn's passport. He began the conversation by pointing out the clear signs of its counterfeit nature. The seal was wide of the mark, the holographic image a complete fake, and the embossed stamp a forgery.

"But how...?" Dunn asked. The moment the words escaped him he knew the answer: Hollis McAllister and her friends. Somewhere in the time between Venice and Greece, Hollis stole his passport and replaced it with a fake. They stole his identity along with credit card numbers, savings account numbers, passcodes and passport, the works. He was suddenly a *persona non grata*, abandoned in a foreign country not of his choosing (after all, he had arrived on a whim) with rapidly dwindling resources.

Inspector Valadon clicked his tongue in reproach of the predicament and shook his head. "You are...how you say...?" He snapped his fingers. "Up dee creek *avec sans* paddle, eh?" He seemed to take great pleasure in Dunn's misfortune. When the writer corrected him—"Up *shit* creek with*out* a paddle"—the inspector's countenance fell into the lifeless mask of the bureaucrat. An impenetrable wall rose between them. Dunn thought, he should have thought twice for correcting the aphorism.

The inspector proceeded to quote the law—chapter, line and verse—to reiterate the gravity of the situation, of visiting the Netherlands without a valid passport. "Do you not know zee consequences facing yourself?" How could the writer possibly appreciate how painful it was for Inspector Valadon to prosecute an American citizen—"a famous *auteur*," he exclaimed with an index finger in the air—during these delicate times of deteriorating international relations? The *delicate times* the inspector referred to were the years proceeding George W. Bush's invasion of Iraq over imaginary weapons of mass destruction and trumped up accusations of participation in terrorism. After the French criticized the president's declared intent to go to war, French fries served in the Capitol cafeteria became known as "freedom fries" and all things French—with the possible exception of the Statue of Liberty, a gift from France—became *verboten*, to forgive the mix of parlance. *Fois gras* was removed from the hors d'oeuvres plates at "K Street" cocktail parties. California Zinfandel Blush and Gallo replaced French Merlot and Sauvignon Blanc. Even presidential candidate John Kerry was not exempt from the slander of a Gaullist ancestry. "This comes at zee worst time, no?" Inspector Valadon exclaimed.

"What will happen to me?" Dunn asked, acquiescing to his fate.

A fingerprint expert entered the room and proceeded to roll each of Dunn's fingers and thumbs on a pad of ink and over a ten-marked rectangle of paper. Meanwhile, the Inspector explained that the *auteur* could not leave the Netherlands; indeed he could not travel by boat, train or by car outside of Amsterdam. The American Consulate would, of course, be notified, and as soon as his identity was verified, his passport would be restored or replaced. Until then, Dunn was a guest of Interpol, forced to reside at a youth hostel, the only choice of residence available at the time. "The department hires zee apartment," the inspector explained, but unfortunately on his rotation through Amsterdam, he was occupying it at the moment. "When I return to Lyons, zen, of course, you may have eet," he said with a lopsided grin. He stood stiffly in an awkward kind of military attention to shake Dunn's sweating hand when two Interpol officers entered the office to escort him to the hostel.

At the office door he hesitated. He wished for further explanation. "What about my laptop, sir, my luggage at the hotel?" A man, it was explained, would be sent to collect and bring them to Interpol where the goods could be safely stored.

"Inspector, does this mean I cannot have my Cashier's Check? I have nothing to live on," Dunn declared.

"No need, Monsieur. No need. You are zee guest of Interpol, until this leetle misunderstanding is, how you say, *feexed*." He patted the plastic envelope in which Dunn's wallet, (fake) passport, and Cashier's Check were to be stored. "We will keep an eye on your possessions. Believe me. Eef they are not safe here, where are they safe, eh?"

And so Dunn, flummoxed, penniless and without his passport, was transported by an Interpol officer to a filthy youth hostel, there to be lodged for the time being. He was given a relatively clean but worn blanket for his cot and shown to his room by the hostel director, a man approximately Dunn's age with a world-class comb over. Dunn would be sharing the dormitory room with German, Italian, French and American males whose lack of hygiene was immediately evident. One of the Americans, a gregarious lad of nineteen, warned Dunn about drinking the water from the tap in the communal bathroom. "It gave me cramps," he told the older man, shaking his hand. "The name's Jason, by the way." He was traveling with his wiener dog, Karlo. Upon introduction, the dog jumped onto Dunn's trousers and began dry humping his leg. The dog repeated this revolting behavior every time he entered the room. A French boy laughed. "Karlo and you are very close, eh?" *A little too close*, Dunn muttered.

He was provided food vouchers, two per day for breakfast and dinner, no lunch. The vouchers were redeemable at a cafeteria-style restaurant across the canal from the hostel. Since European breakfast consisted of espresso and a croissant, Dunn saved the breakfast voucher for lunch. He ate his dinners at the restaurant as late in the day as he could possibly stand, prolonging the meal, delaying for as long as possible his return to the non-aromatic hostel.

The restaurant was run by an Arab-looking gentleman and his family, slender girls in their late twenties and early thirties dressed in silk *khalats* and caftans. They had identical dark satiny hair worn long and tied in ponytails. Considering the current situation in the Middle East, Dunn kept his nationality to himself, speaking in a slurred French Canadian accent, not to give his American roots away. During the first week of this new routine, in the evening the eldest daughter approached and asked if he was an American. "Non," Dunn said. "I am Canadians. Quebec." It seemed to satisfy her. From that night forward, he received smiles of welcome and free cups of coffee from the owner, Samir Arslan of Southern Lebanon.

Samir Arslan was Druze and had escaped after the long civil war in Lebanon that preceded the Israeli invasion in the 1980s. Dunn grew to like Samir, liked him very much. He was an oasis in a desert of exile. As Dunn visited the restaurant night after night, their acquaintance gradually matured into friendship, and eventually he was forced to confess. "I am not Canadian, Samir, I am sorry to say," Dunn told the restaurateur. Samir slapped him on the back and smiled. "I know this, not to worry."

"You *knew* I was American?"

"Of course. It is obvious."

"If it's any consolation," Dunn said, "I didn't vote for George Bush."

"The elder or younger?"

"Neither."

Once, they shared half a bottle of red wine to celebrate the end of the day. When Dunn asked if he had ever considered returning home (a desire to return home being on his mind day and night), the restaurateur replied, "Not until the world to give up on war, my friend. Until then..." He smiled and poured another glass. "I enjoy you company and the peace of Amsterdam for my daughters, Allah Akba!" Artillery shells, Dunn later learned, had killed his wife in August of 1982, six hours *after* the negotiated cease-fire between the PLO and the invading army of Ariel Sharon.

Samir and the writer of mystery novels became good friends. On one particular evening after the wine flowed freely, Dunn told Samir his story, beginning with the long weekend in New York City, of boarding the Northern Star, meeting Audrey, Hollis, and Stanley, getting ripped off in Greece through his own hubris and stupidity. Samir was very sympathetic. His facial expression mirrored the ups and downs of the confession. He smirked at Dunn's good fortune for bedding such a beautiful young woman. He wept when he heard about the "*sharmuta* bitch" stealing his friend's identity and savings account. "What can I do to help you?" he asked, drying his eyes on his apron. Dunn shook Samir's hand and said that he would like to use his computer to wire a couple thousand dollars from friends in New York. "I don't have a bank account in the Netherlands, Samir. I would need to have it wired to your account."

This simple request terribly disappointed Samir in his new friend. He knew about the Nigerian Scam. He had not fallen off the tuna boat yesterday, he said. He'd heard this all before but had not expected deceptions from the man he was beginning to consider as a brother. (Dunn had no idea he felt this way.) Anger swelled the cords in his neck, and his golden skin darkened beneath his eyes. Before his fury was further inflamed, Dunn assured him that all transactions would take place between banks. He would have nothing to do with the transfer. To sweeten the deal, Dunn offered to pay him two hundred euros (his eyebrows rose) upon conclusion of the transaction. Samir would have complete control of the deal. He would make the telephone calls to New York City ("I'll reimburse the cost," Dunn said) and he would accept the calls from the writer's agent, Glenda. During the process, if anything struck him as fishy, he could back out of the deal; he could cancel the agreement at any time during the course of negotiations. "Are we agreed?"

Samir poured two glasses of sauterne. He took his sweet time to admire the thick yellowy liquid in the light fixtures of his restaurant. He squinted at the writer and nodded his head once. "I have complete control? You give me phone number for bank? You have nothing to doing with it? And once ended, you give me three hundred euros?"

"Two hundred," he corrected with a smile and a clink of his glass.

He shrugged and took a sip of wine, granting his mistake in arithmetic but knowing full well that he was in the catbird's seat. "Deal," he said. And they drank on it, drank until long past midnight. After Samir had fallen asleep in a chair, Dunn sneaked into the back room and logged online on the restaurant computer. He sent several messages to Glenda and his San Francisco lawyer. He wrote to his financial adviser. "Secure my accounts," Dunn wrote. "Or else!" Glenda, he knew, would be relieved to hear from him after almost a two-week silence. Dunn was in luck. Glenda had been online, and she responded immediately. What could she do to move the process along? How much do you need? Is two grand enough? Dunn assured her that it might be a slow process with his new friend Samir Arslan, but not to worry, he was an honest soul with a good heart, an ally. Dunn thanked her and said she'd hear from him soon. He logged off and walked across the street to sleep in his bunk at the hostel for a few hours before he would have to get up and face another day as a homeless rube, an old Ragged Dick.

Chapter Six

To FURTHER CLARIFY how far along Interpol was in their investigation of his identity and travel fund theft, Dunn telephoned Valadon once a week but the Inspector never took his calls. He was always "out of *zee* office." How was it possible for the man to be out of the office every time he called? "Let me ask you," Dunn shouted into the public telephone to be heard above the hubbub at the hostel, above the cacophony of rock music played on half a dozen boom boxes—it was how Dunn imagined Babel must have sounded. "May I come by to pick up a change of clothes?" This was not allowed, he was told. "At least, a change of undergarments?" Evidently, this too was prohibited. At the end of each call, Dunn left a message with the Dutch officers whose thick accents were impossible to comprehend. The officers inspired no confidence that the messages were ever delivered as sent.

And so life took a left turn for the writer of mysteries. Fate had seemingly abandoned him to the Furies. He spent his imposed leisure as productively as he could, waiting for resolution, waiting for Glenda to forward cash via Samir's bank account. Oddly enough, his deplorable circumstances inspired him to begin writing again, but without his laptop, he was forced to rely on the analog means of inscription: pencil and paper. He borrowed lined paper from the hostel director, but when this was no longer offered, he wrote on Samir's restaurant napkins and on the backs of cash register receipts. He rolled the scraps of paper together and held them with a rubber band, bits and pieces of a novel that he was having difficulty organizing in his mind, character sketches and descriptions of Amsterdam's side streets and slack canals, ideas for plotting and points of view. The discipline of writing was the only thing that saved his sanity, that and his budding friendship with Samir Arslan.

Bob Dunn lived a life of the mind, as most writers must. Mysteries were his forte. When he was writing, *really* writing, the novels took on a flesh of their own. It wasn't so much that he confused his fictions with reality; he wasn't crazy. But reality can be as fickle as identity. There were delicious moments during the Atlantic crossing when he truly believed himself Ashley Winslow, daring, debonair, lover of young women, not Bob Dunn, divorced white middle-aged man with a mediocre publishing career behind him. Now, alone and broke in Amsterdam under the auspices of Interpol, he felt totally confused as to who and what he really was. The applecart of his identity had been overturned.

A confused identity may have something to do with the metamorphosis children undergo on their way to maturity. We are born small, helpless. We learn to crawl, to speak, tell time and tie our shoes. We graduate from high school, and we think we're grown up until we enter college or the army where legions of superiors tell us differently. Perhaps our undeveloped identity originates in childhood as a dispensable organ like the appendix, only to become something permanent, mystifying and arthritic as we age.

As children, we put on costumes to play cowboys and Indians. As teenagers we try on personality styles as though window-shopping for a new wardrobe. In childhood we fully believe that we turn into the characters we play, and as adults we become our job, our profession, our role in the social theater. The world expects from adults a degree of stability and responsibility. We are instructed to be solid citizens, to do the right thing. "Don't kid around," people say. An old friend of Dunn's, an anthropologist, once told him that this corrective behavior, this socialization of the young, was meant to insure the continuation of the species. Had our primate ancestors amused themselves by pretending to be something other than hominids struggling to survive, we simply wouldn't have. People must *find themselves* to stay alive. This was what the anthropologist taught his college students, to be true to themselves.

Dunn envied the anthropologist for the immediate pleasure of his audience, whereas being a writer was a solitary profession whose audience was more or less invisible. Had anyone invited Dunn to speak at a respected forum or literary gathering, he would have jumped at the opportunity. He often imagined himself at a podium, the audience filled with past PEN presidents and Pulitzers, hanging on his every word as he cited passages from Kafka, Flaubert, Hemingway, and Maupassant; as he tossed off bon mots; as he recited lines from Yeats ("The worst are full of passionate intensity....") and T. S. Eliot ("Let us go then, you and I, when the evening is spread out against the sky...."), and tied all of it together and related it to his Max Sledge Mysteries. He would have outlined themes in great literature and read passages of dialogue from renowned writers, and drawn parallels to his own work. This was the fantasy of Ashley Winslow, a sobriquet that accompanied Dunn everywhere he went. Members of his imaginary audience might well have asked, "Who *are* you then, Ashley Winslow or Max Sledge?" He would have been loath to reply, "Neither. I'm Bob Dunn."

In Amsterdam, at the youth hostel, an imposed leisure forced serious introspection upon him. *What have I become?* In the lateness of life, he realized how little he knew about himself. *Am I my alter ego?* He had written thirty-two Max Sledge Mysteries. At book signings—rare as they were—on the inside cover he wrote, *All the best, Ashley Winslow.* When he gave the occasional talk to the Vacaville Women's Literary League, the attendees addressed him as Mr. Winslow. So, who was he? Was he Ash, the European traveler, seducer of blithe young women? Or was he Bob Dunn, a mediocre novelist? Alfred Jarrey, the French absurdist playwright, said, "Wear the mask long enough and you become the mask."

Dunn was unsure who he was, but he was certain of one thing: he was a victim. No doubt about it.

When he was a kid growing up in San Leandro, California, the neighborhood boys used to play "War," a variation of Cowboys and Indians with automatic weapons. After choosing up sides, there was always a mean kid on the other team who imagined a slight or insult of Dunn's that bound them to vengeance. Or it might have been that they just didn't like the way Bobby Dunn looked. He was a skinny kid and therefore vulnerable as an early casualty in the game of War. He was not unlike the radio operator figurine in a bag of plastic green army men, the squatting soldier that could barely stand up, the one that didn't have a rifle pointed at the enemy. The radio operator was the most vulnerable and expendable piece in any kid's collection of plastic green army men. When the boys played War, Dunn automatically became the equivalent of the radio operator. It didn't take an insult to muster up animosity for him. All it took was one look at his scrawny hide.

The boys would line up, the two armies in a field, gripping their weapons (toy guns of one stripe or another), as a means of measuring the opponent. Most of the time, a kid known as Wanker pointed Dunn out among the line of prepubescent infantry. Sometimes Wanker would pair up with another kid to single him out and "kill" him. And the killing was not benign, meaning the quaint imitation of gunfire boys make and the melodramatic way their victims "die." Wanker's manner of "killing" was more real than performance art. Sometimes he came at Bobby Dunn with rocks and sticks. Dunn remembered getting hit on the side of the face with a stone thrown by Wanker or one of his cronies. It was dangerous business, playing War.

This experience made him wonder, lying on his cot and staring at the water-stained ceiling in the hostel, when he'd been draft age back in 1966, had he been drafted into the real American army (instead of attending college for the student deferment) and sent to Vietnam, would Dunn have been picked out for special treatment by a Vietnamese Wanker? He could imagine the Vietcong sizing him up through field glasses. "Ah, the skinny kid. He'll be my first kill." Had he been born in a previous era, had he fought in his ancestral homeland—Scotland on his father's side or Sweden on his mother's— would he have stood in a line of warriors facing the enemy, his face stained in blue mud? If so, some goober from the other side would have chosen him among the hoard as a target for his wrath. The horns would blare, they would charge the field, and poor old Dunn would be down and out with a spear through the guts because some Wanker on the other side got it into his noggin that he didn't like him. Didn't like him one bit.

This, he reasoned, was what had happened aboard ship. Hollis and her friends hadn't known him, but they recognized him for what he was, a natural victim. They'd singled him out as a special case for their diabolical plot to steal his money and identity.

"I'm not sure," Dunn said softly to himself. "But I think nice guys finish last." *Nice guys* like Bob Dunn pretty much stood out in a crowd as the likely first candidate to suffer the slings and arrows of outrageous fortune.

And lying there in all that gloom, Dunn thought about what it had felt like to fall in love for the first time since Marjorie had dumped him. Love for Dunn did not come along very often. In fact, it was as rare as hens' teeth.

Back in high school, he hoped that his classmates saw him as a reasonably good-looking guy. Dunn got it wrong. As the schoolgirls phrased it, "He's not unreasonably bad looking but…." He did not attend either his Junior or Senior Proms, and he only dated rarely. His first official date had been with Marjorie. Now that he was categorically old—closing in on sixty—he knew his days of wine and roses were over. "I have heard the mermaids singing, each to each. I do not think that they will sing to me." He would grow old and wear his trousers rolled.

What did any of this matter now?

In the early afternoons on most days, Dunn found himself wasting time beneath Samir Arslan's restaurant awning, enviously eyeing tourists burdened by their shopping parcels, watching the carefree teenagers and the well-to-do "slumming" through the older districts of Amsterdam. He was not a person that anyone paid much attention to. He had stopped shaving every day and had neglected his hygiene. He wore the same shirt and pants day in and day out, resembling the homeless alcoholics who haunted the canals. He stopped caring about his looks, stopped caring that is until one rain-soaked afternoon at Samir's restaurant he saw a vision of hope jogging down the cobblestones wearing black Spandex shorts and a sweat top.

It was Audrey of the thieving Hollis Gang. No question about it. He knew that derriere as well as the back of his hand.

Dunn's heart skipped a beat. What should he do? Should he chase and accost her? Surely, nothing but further humiliation at the hands of the Amsterdam police would come from that. Should he ring up Interpol? "A lot of good that'll do," he said to himself. In any case, he would have to make up his mind soon because Audrey was running away.

Dunn got out of the chair and went into the street. He gazed at the figure retreating along the side of the canal, beneath the spare limbs of tulip trees. The rain had stopped. A motorbike whizzed past from behind, startling Dunn to his senses. At last, he took off after the girl at a jogger's pace.

She was making her way up De Wittenkade toward Westerpark, this he assumed, along a minor canal clotted by tourist barges. On account of his age and physical ineptitude, Dunn kept a good distance back so as not to be spotted. Still, the runner was forced to halt at an intersection where a main thoroughfare crossed the canal by an auto bridge, waiting for the traffic lights to change. To avoid being seen, he ducked into a florist's shop where he was at a loss to explain his presence, more or less irritating the clerk, a round ball of a woman in a floral dress who reeked of camphor and cigarettes and who shooed him away with a straw broom.

Audrey was across the intersection now and running at a faster clip. Dunn mustered all that he had left in him just to keep up. By the time they independently reached the end of the straat, Dunn was out of breath, drained of reserves and sweating like a glass of iced tea on a summer porch. To his surprise, Westerpark was not Audrey's destination. The cobbled street did a U-turn over a bridge, near Haarlemmerweg, circling back along the opposite side of the canal. As Dunn clambered up the footbridge to De Wittenkade on the north side, he glanced up at his prey only to see her running in place, glaring, no more than five meters away. Was it the flash of recognition in her eyes or was she registering annoyance with the mysterious old man on her tail?

She answered Dunn's dilemma by flipping him off and returning to her afternoon jog, clearly annoyed but indifferent to his perverted behavior and enfeebled pursuit. She decided that he was harmless enough. Let the old man try to chase her to look at her well-sculpted ass, what did she care?

As she ran off, he realized his appearance had fallen into such a disreputable state no one from his immediate past could have identified him.

He kept in the hunt at a more respectful distance, careful not to tweak her ire but determined not to lose sight of her.

Dunn discovered that Audrey resided in a flat in a four-story building less than a kilometer from Samir Arslan's restaurant, on a straat named after someone called Fannius Scholten, an obscure writer of the early 19th century. Dunn stood across the street hidden by the shelter of shadows and tulip trees as he continued to spy on her building for another hour.

When he was about to give up and return to the hostel, having memorized her address to come back at another time when, perhaps, he might find the courage to confront her, Audrey and her co-conspirators, Stanley Bledsoe, and Holister Ehrlich in the arms of the same boy who'd approached them on the Greek isle, obviously not a stranger but her lover, came bouncing down the front steps, on their way out by all appearances, the four dressed in finery purchased with Dunn's vacation funds, laughing without a care in the world.

Stepping back into the evening shadows as the rain began to fall again, Dunn muttered to himself, "That's right. Laugh, you bastards. Soon you'll be singing a different tune, I can assure you." And off he went in the opposite direction to tell his friend Samir about this coincidental discovery.

✉   ✉   ✉

"What we need do, my friend," Samir told him over a glass of Port, "is kidnap her."

It was after hours. The restaurant was shuttered and most lights switched off. The girls had finished stacking chairs on the tables and had mopped the floor, leaving their father and his peculiar friend alone to argue politics or do whatever old men did late at night. A half-empty bottle of cheap Port sat on the only occupied table in the place, illuminated by a security light burning in the kitchen.

"Kidnap her?" Dunn remarked. "You've got to be joking."

"No, is no joke. Look, my friend, is only way you get your money returned to you." Samir went on to explain that in the Middle East, Saudi Arabia in particular, kidnapping was commonplace as a means to settling scores, a way to shed bad blood.

"I can't kidnap the girl. What if they've destroyed all the evidence linking their crime to me? The police will arrest *me*. What if they're armed? What if—?"

"Oh what if this, what if that," the restaurateur mocked. He leaned forward to pour another finger of Port in both glasses. "You cannot live life on what if's. You must take the pants, as they say."

Some of his friend's expressions confused Dunn when they drank together. He often muttered rough translations of ancient Lebanese sayings that made no sense.

"Pants?"

"Yes, of course," he said, chortling. "You, famous writer, sure you know, eh? It is Latin. *Carpe denim*. You must take the pants." He squeezed his fist in the air.

After a moment, Dunn corrected him. "*Carpe diem* is what you mean. Seize the day, not the pants, Samir."

The Druze shrugged. "Whatever. It matters not. Still, you must kidnap girl, this *assassin*, to show you mean business." He went on to explain in detail what must be done. "You American agent, she send you money, eh?"

Dunn nodded as he patted the wad of euros in his jacket pocket. "Yes, thank you, Samir." Glenda had been true to her word. Earlier that morning, she'd wired a thousand dollars to Samir's bank account, and now over Port the two men were settling their accounts to everyone's satisfaction.

Samir's eyes twinkled. "Yes, and I am two hundred euros richer, eh?"

Dunn sighed and took a sip from his glass.

"So, now you have…what you call it…wear it all."

"*Wear it all…?*"

"Yes."

Dunn thought for a moment. "You mean *wherewithal?*"

He nodded. "Bribe the officials, and take out your enemies. You can even the tide." He smiled knowingly at another confusing malapropism. "It is time to take your revenge, my friend. Not sit around here all day looking like a depressed dog."

"Samir," Dunn began but found himself exhausted from his impromptu jog earlier in the day. The alcohol coursed through his veins and was deadening his mind. "My friend, I should go to bed. I'm beat."

Samir got up and circled the table to slap his friend on the back. "Yes, yes. Time to lock up and go make love someone's wife." He laughed. "But listen to what I have to say just once. Take the money. Use it. I don't know how, but make those assassins pay for how they did to you. You must act like a man and stand up."

Dunn agreed with Samir and from his seat he shook his hand.

"No, my friend, you don't understand. You must stand up. I no make joke. It is time to go home."

Back at the hostel and once in bed, surrounded by drunken snoring boys, Dunn's mind began to range over Samir's suggestion that he consider kidnapping Audrey. Surely her jog along the canal was part of a regular exercise program. She would be at it again, if not tomorrow then the next day, and Dunn would be waiting for her. But he must act soon. How long could she and her companions be expected, now flush with thousands in cash from Dunn's "vacation account," to stay in Amsterdam when the whole of Europe beckoned? A plot was hatched in the recesses of his brain before he fell into dreamless sleep.

On the following day, Dunn waited in his usual chair beneath Samir Arslan's awning, but Audrey was a no-show. He sat there all day without gaining any sense of achievement. Later, he retreated to the hostel to nurse a deepening despair. Perhaps, like most young people, repetition bored Audrey, and instead of taking a familiar route, she had decided on a different course each day. This fly in the ointment might force a change in plans, and rather than kidnap her, Dunn would be forced to arm himself and confront the perpetrators at their residence. This is what crossed his mind as he tried to shut out the odors and distractions of living among youthful world travelers on the cheap.

"Tomorrow," Dunn repeated to himself. "We shall see."

Tomorrow proved ripe. Audrey in black Spandex and a tank top jogged past the restaurant at exactly six minutes past noon, and she did again the following day at the same time. *She's as reliable*, Dunn mused, *as a fascist train*.

Despite her cooperation in the enterprise, Dunn had no clue as to how to proceed in the kidnapping. He made no plans for her imprisonment, if it came to that, or for her disposal. How was he supposed to contact her friends with his demands? None of it had been thought through, and this bothered Dunn. It was the worst of times, in a real-life situation, to suffer writer's block. His imagination had failed him.

That evening when Samir served him dinner, Dunn paid with a few extra euros now that he had the cash (thanks to Glenda). For the first time in their short friendship, Samir saw that the American wore clean clothes. His hair was combed and the whiskers were shaved from his chin. The Druze said, "You lookin' good. Are you happy?"

"Thank you, Samir. Yes, yes, I guess you could say I'm happy."

Standing there and wiping his hands on his apron, Samir considered Dunn for a moment or two. Finally, he said, "You saw her today, did you no?"

Dunn glanced up. He wasn't sure how to respond. The whole idea of kidnapping a person had seized the gears of his mind.

"And yet, you do nothing, is that right? Look, I have something for you." He looked behind and saw that the surrounding tables were indeed empty. Then he reached into the fold of his apron and pulled out a semi-automatic handgun. "Take it," he said in a seditious whisper.

"I can't take that."

"Take it! It's not real gun, you old fool." Samir laughed.

Dunn saw that it was a toy. He accepted the gift and slipped it into his pants pocket.

"Where'd you get this…?"

"It was my son's." A tear came to the old man's eyes, and Dunn considered the possibility that his friend had lost both wife and his only son to a bombing raid in Lebanon.

"In a country full of weapons, no son a mine is to play army with so terrible a thing. I took it from him. Now you take it. Take it, and when she run by tomorrow you follow her and when the coast is queer, as they say, you come up behind and shove it right here, above the second rib. Where Allah took Adam's rib to make woman, you understand?"

Dunn nodded, his heart rate rising, sweat forming on his brow and his dinner getting cold.

"Okay, but what do I do after…?"

Samir took an empty chair and pulled it close to his friend. He leaned forward and spoke in a whisper. "I own building, not far, with how-you-say fundament."

"*Fundament?*"

Samir thought carefully for a second. "Basement. It is *basement*, I think. Forgive me. Anyway, you take her and tie her up. I leave you rope, only the best. Lebanese rope." The restaurateur winked.

Dunn's old heart skipped a beat. "Where is this place?"

Samir leaned closer. "I write address on receipt." He gestured at the bill, and Dunn took a quick look. On the back of the receipt was the address of a building not far from the restaurant, on De Wittenkade.

"You take out your weapon and tell her to make note. Say she kidnap and ransom is...how much they steal from you?"

"Over twenty thousand dollars American."

"Piece of pie!" He snapped his fingers. "Ransom twenty thousand dollars. You know where she live, right? Okay, you drop off note. This, I assure you, will settle the matter. Now, I must to get back my customer. Eat, my friend. Enjoy!"

How could Dunn eat? He felt the impression of the plastic toy gun against his thigh. Did he have the guts to do what Samir had suggested, kidnap Audrey and tie her up in a basement? As his doubts began to pile up like cordwood, one of the girls brought him a complimentary glass of red wine, something Italian from the Alto Adige, perhaps an Amarone, for it was high in alcohol and rich as syrup. After he drank it down to settle the nerves, the girl brought another.

Soon, Dunn began to accept what he must do if he ever hoped to get his passport back and the return of his fortune.

Chapter Seven

IT SOON BECAME CLEAR if Dunn were to pull off this caper in the manner of Max Sledge, a disguise would be necessary. He spent the next morning exploring a costume kiosk at the food center at Groothandelsmarkt. An overweight man in a lawn chair, his dirty T-shirt barely covering a bulging belly, ran a flea market of sorts for clothing on consignment. Dunn could not understand the man's Dutch, and he spoke only English phrases, and so communication was achieved through pantomime. The overweight man gestured at gypsy dresses, which Dunn declined, and pushed an outfit suitable to Abraham Lincoln probably because he presumed correctly that the customer was American. What Dunn was looking for was something less obnoxious and more dignified, yet unique; something that would allow him to blend in with the general population (tourist or otherwise) living in the district in Amsterdam. He settled on a pair of black slacks, an overcoat with pockets to hide the plastic gun, motorcycle boots that fit perfectly, and a felt hat typical of the Dutch.

When it came time to pay for the hat, the proprietor declared, "Ten euro," and held up his fingers.

"What?!"

"Look. Zsofia Marx." He rubbed his fingers together to indicate how precious it was, this Zsofia Marx-designed felt hat.

Dunn paid the man but believed he'd been cheated on the hat.

Still, it was critical to the overall disguise he had in mind for the next day.

At precisely fifteen minutes before noon, Bob Dunn in his disguise that only a sleuth such as Max Sledge would wear stood out from under Samir Arslan's awning, away from the lunch crowd. Wearing sunglasses that he'd stolen from a drunken kid at the youth hostel, Dunn was not even recognized by his Druze friend. He had to flag Samir down as he shuttled trays of food from table to table. "How may I help, sir?" Samir said. In a whisper, Dunn said, "It's me." Surprised but containing his oversight, Samir pursed his lips and said with a smile, "I knew it was you. All over this time."

Just then a female jogger appeared at the top of the straat. It was Audrey.

Dunn swallowed to fortify his courage and waited, his hand on the fake weapon in the pocket of the coat. As he stood waiting, he wished it had been a real gun.

When she reached the outside terrace of the restaurant, Dunn pulled the felt hat down over his eyes and looked in the opposite direction as he stepped off the curb. His motorcycle boots clunked against the cobblestones and reverberated up through the top of his head. As he swung his arms, the long coat swished awkwardly from side to side. She was getting away. Dunn gathered up his courage, pressed forward, and in two or three strides, he was beside her.

The disguise was useless. She recognized him as the old bearded pervert who had stalked her over the past week. She stopped, arms akimbo, catching her breath. They stood staring at one another, Dunn frozen in a kind of giddy paralysis, she clearly pissed off. Finally, she declared, "What the fuck do you want, old man?"

Hearing the expletive shocked Dunn out of his paralysis. He pulled the weapon, pausing long enough for her to see what it was, before he shoved it into her side as Samir had suggested. She gave a high-pitched yelp that her fear muffled into a hopeless sob.

"Do as I say and you won't get hurt. Do you understand?" Dunn said.

She nodded.

"Come with me. Walk slowly. Make no drastic moves. If you try to run away, I will shoot you. Understood?"

Again, she nodded.

As they walked in tandem toward Samir's building, Dunn began to feel elated at the power he held over the girl. This was something as a writer of novels he'd written about many times, but to actually experience it almost overwhelmed the emotions.

Samir's building was a two-story warehouse constructed of stone, it's windows blotted by old yellow newspapers. It was a foreboding place that caused Audrey to stiffen. "Please. You don't have to do this."

In character now, he said, "Shut the fuck up," just as some of the bad guys did in his Max Sledge Mysteries.

They entered the old building from the back through a wooden door that creaked when shut behind them. There was insufficient light but just enough to guide them down a short flight of stairs to a sheet metal door punctuated with black rivets. Dunn opened it and shoved his hostage into Samir's basement. At this moment, Audrey was crying uncontrollably, which nearly drained him of resolve. He was close to forfeiting the entire scheme and letting her go.

But then he remembered how she and the others had deceived him onboard the Northern Star and plotted to rip off his lifesavings.

"Why are you doing this? Who. Are. You?" she cried haltingly.

"Turn around," he demanded.

Quickly, he wound the Lebanese rope tightly around her wrists—"That's too tight!"—and sat her down in a folding chair to which he bound her ankles. He wrapped the last of the rope over her exposed thighs, as the Spandex had ridden up, and tied the ends to a galvanized pipe that ran across the stone floor.

Finally, he faced her. She looked up at the imposing figure in motorcycle boots, overcoat and funny hat. Even in the basement darkness, he wore a very cool pair of Ray-Ban Wayfarers, something her boyfriend Stanley would have worn. He seemed nervous which worsened her sense of fear that his intentions were totally wicked.

"Look," she said. "If you want me to have sex with you, you're gonna have to loosen the ropes—"

"I don't want anything of the kind. Not with you, and never again with your friend."

"What're you talking about?"

The second Dunn said "never again with your friend," he knew he had perhaps exposed his true identity, something he'd been keen on concealing. But Audrey was not a very observant girl, and the mistake cost him nothing. She was clueless.

"I'm not going to hurt you," he said at last.

"Well, you already hurt me. You're killing my wrists." She looked down. "My ankles'll never be the same."

Dunn was beginning to wish he'd brought along a sack to put over her head and a gag for her mouth.

"If you don't want sex, what do you want?"

Dunn removed his notebook from a coat pocket and ripped off a blank sheet of paper. He clicked his ballpoint and handed the implements to her before realizing she couldn't possibly have accepted them. Her hands were tied.

He blinked at the stupidity, scolding himself for poor planning.

"I want you to write a note to your friends," he said.

"How do you know my friends?"

"Silence!" he shouted a little unconvincingly but loud enough to ring their ears. "You've taken advantage of a friend of mine. Stolen a great deal of money. Inconvenienced him. Do you understand what I'm saying to you?"

She nodded, and the realization just then clarified in her mind as she remembered back to seeing the old pervert that first time he had followed her, when she'd stopped him at the footbridge. There'd been something familiar about him that she'd not been able to put her finger on, but now she knew. It was the old guy. Max Sledge or whatever.

"You're Max Sledge, aren't you?" she said.

Dunn repeated in his mind, *The jig is up.*

It was the mark from the boat, Audrey was sure of it, the one she didn't have to screw. This time she'd been the one to draw the longer straw. She'd been relieved to let Holister play the "love interest" this time around. He wasn't too bad looking but he was so *old.* Whenever Audrey drew the short straw and had to sleep with the mark, it drove Stanley crazy with jealousy. It took weeks to convince Stanley that she still loved him and that it had been a sacrifice to screw some old bastard in order to steal him blind.

But here was something completely different. Ordinarily, the marks did little more than contact their banks, credit card companies, and the local police or Interpol. They never chased her down or confronted her with a semi-automatic, for God's sake. Staring down the barrel of the old man's gun, Audrey wondered if she ought to consider a change in careers.

"It doesn't matter."

"What doesn't matter?" she asked.

"It doesn't matter, you know who I am. It changes nothing. I'm going to untie one of your hands now, and you're going to write a note," he said. "Are you right- or left-handed?"

"Left."

"Okay." He gently loosened the rope to allow her to slip out her left hand, and for an instant Audrey thought about slamming her fist into his face but the feel of the gun pressing against her breast drained away the gumption. He handed her the piece of paper and pen.

"What should I write?"

Dunn wanted to say something Max Sledge would have said, something like, *Well, I don't want you to write me a novel, if that's what you think.* But he thought better for it. "I want you to write to your friends. Tell them you've been kidnapped and held for ransom. That's right. Tell them they need to pay back the money they stole from me, do you understand? Twenty grand and my passport. You can keep the credit card numbers. They're useless."

She began to write. "I can hardly see."

"Write the note," Dunn said in his best Max Sledge.

"What if they don't do as you say?"

Dunn, fully in the role of his alter ego, straightened his shoulders and cocked his head. "If they don't accede to my demands..."

"Accede? What's that mean?" she asked.

He cleared his throat. "If they don't do what I say..."

In that moment Dunn lost all impetus. How could he convincingly tell this beautiful girl that, if her friends didn't do what he told them to do, he would be forced to kill her? It was all such a charade. The house of cards collapsed around him; he could feel it. Not even inertia could drive him forward from here.

"What did you say?" Audrey asked, sensing vulnerability in the old man's voice.

"You know goddamned well what'll happen," Dunn said at last, having been saved in the end by the ghost of Max Sledge. For emphasis, he pressed the nose of the gun into her flesh.

She began to write furiously and soon asked for another sheet.

✉   ✉   ✉

"So," Samir asked, "have you prepared a drop site for the ransom money?"

"Drop site?"

They were at their usual table after hours, a bottle of Greek Retsina between them, something Dunn was having difficulty getting used to drinking.

"Don't tell. You no do this thing? You, writer mysterious books, you no plan a drop site? What're you, crazy?"

"Samir, I've never done this before. I don't know where you got the idea that I was some big time sleuth or something." Dunn was exhausted by events of the day, not able to stop worrying about the young woman he'd left tied up in a basement, a few hundred meters from where they sat.

"Okay, okay. You need help, no shit. Listen to me. Listen to me!"

For a second, Dunn thought Samir was going to slap him.

"You already deliver note, right? So, they get it. Now the assassin know. The brood of vipers they squirming, eh? So, you gotta plan a drop site, where they gone leave your random money…"

"Ransom money," Dunn corrected.

"Right. See, now you catch on. Now you understand how Samir do things, eh?"

"I could go to prison for the rest of my life." Dunn shook his head and stared blankly at the empty restaurant, the worn tables looking pitiful. "I think I'm going to just let her go. Tomorrow…"

"What you say? No. Samir not let you do this." He slammed his open hand on the table, and their cups danced. Dunn faced his friend. "I knew this happen. I knew. You silly American, you can no do one simple thing, eh? How you get so rich, so big, you Americani, you *Ghabans* with tanks and jets? How you *Muti* get so rich, eh?" He shook his head. "I take care this thing for you, my friend. Relax. I take care." And he poured Dunn the last of the Retsina.

The hangover from the resinated wine was the worst in Dunn's life. It felt as though his head were in a vise every time one of the college-aged boys at the hostel shouted or played his hip-hop nonsense loudly on a boom box. To escape the cacophony,

Dunn took a walk to Westerpark and sat in the northern sunlight to let the toxins sweat out of him. The skin of his arm smelled like tree pitch. Samir had poisoned him.

By noon, he made it back to the restaurant where he was coaxed into having a sandwich and Heineken. The beer did the trick. His thoughts clarified, and before finishing the cold cuts, he hurried off to check on his hostage, which he'd neglected all morning.

Dunn found Audrey asleep, still tied to the chair although she'd managed over the course of the night to loosen the rope. Her exertions had marked the stone floor in a short radius around the galvanized pipe. As he tightened the ropes, she awakened with a start. "Good morning," he said.

"Fuck you, you bastard."

"Well, there's no call for profanity."

"No call...?"

Again, Dunn wished he'd remembered to bring a sack and gag. He was making a mental note when she screamed.

"What?" he said.

"I'm starving. I'm dying down here. You left me alone with no water, no food. Jesus. There're rats and all kinds of creepy shit that comes out at night. You fucker!"

Again, here was something Dunn had not considered, being new to the kidnapping game. He excused himself—Audrey screaming at the top of her lungs as he left—and returned half an hour later with the remains of his lunch and bread along with bottled water to last her two, maybe three days. She drank with abandon and ate ravenously, with Dunn holding the bottled water and feeding the cold cuts to her. In the end, calmer now, she managed to thank him.

"You're welcome," Dunn said. "Look, as soon as this is settled, I'll let you go. As soon as your colleagues come up with the money and meet my demands you can go home. Or wherever it is you wish to go. Greece perhaps or Italy." He giggled. He was feeling a bit giddy from the beer, making nonchalant remarks.

"Look, Max…or whatever your name is," Audrey said. "Look, this can't go on, okay? I know them. My *colleagues* as you say. They're not gonna cough up the cash, okay? They're all in Southern France by now, on their way to Morocco probably. I know them. They're greasers, okay? They ain't gonna cooperate. Not ever."

"But," Dunn began, "you're their friend. You're boyfriend…"

"Stanley?"

"Surely he cares enough to do what I've demanded. Surely."

She shook her head.

He was stunned. This was something he had not considered as a possibility.

"So, you're not really gonna shoot me, are you?" She was doing her best to smile but her lips were trembling and her mouth was so dry her teeth snagged on the upper lip.

Dunn rolled his eyes when he realized he'd left the toy gun at the hostel. "What choice do I have?" he asked, sounding as close to Max Sledge as possible. "You give me no choice."

Tears rolled down her cheeks as her rough exterior over a lifetime of abuse and maltreatment broke down to expose the frightened little girl beneath. Dunn felt sorry for her, sorry for putting her through this ordeal. It wasn't really her fault, he was thinking. His complaint was with Hollis, or whatever her name was, and Stanley, the coldhearted weasel whom Dunn suspected was the mastermind behind the whole operation.

Dunn dabbed her eyes with his handkerchief and let Audrey blow her nose.

"You don't seem like the kind of guy who could kill someone," she said.

"Don't kid yourself," Dunn replied, although she'd touched on the Achilles heal of his plan. There was no way he could bring harm to the girl let alone murder her. Besides, he reminded himself, his so-called weapon was a toy pistol.

"I have to go. I'll be back later with more food."

"Where're you going?"

"I'm going to check on your friends. If they have indeed flown the coop, well, then we must resort to Plan B, won't we?"

"Plan B?"

He formed his hand into a gun and shot his forehead while making a little *bang* in his throat. Terror, he knew, was powerfully persuasive. Even if he didn't get his money and passport back, at least he'd have the satisfaction of knowing he'd caused one of the culprits to suffer a few miserable days in a cold basement.

Loitering outside their apartment and "armed" with Samir's toy gun, Dunn knew that his luck had changed for the better. The Hollis Gang had not left town. There was a lot of activity at the apartment building, but no evidence of the police. Stanley and the Greek boy came and left at a high frequency. They ran back and forth on errands seemingly, carrying bags of groceries into the apartment or six-packs of beer, smoking cigarettes like locomotives.

Clearly, Dunn had upset the beehive.

"So, what is happen with you 'project'?" Samir asked later that night.

"Everything's falling into place," Dunn replied. He gave details of what he'd seen while on surveillance, the hasty comings and goings. "After everything quieted down, I left another note. This one specifying where to leave the ransom." When Samir asked after the hostage, Dunn again registered his qualms and doubts. "If it doesn't work...if they should decide to go to the police...I will have to let her go and run for cover."

Samir patted his friend's knee. "You can stay with my cousin, no problem."

"Where?"

"Beirut."

Dunn said, "Oh, how nice."

At evening's end, Samir told Dunn that he was going to get more personally involved in the caper. "I done want your money, Robert. I do this on principle." He'd agreed to surveil the apartment, taking a day off from the restaurant to do so. He would confront Stanley and the Greek boy when they came outside on an errand. But to do so, he would have to borrow his son's toy gun to "strike fear in their infidel hearts."

"Sure," Dunn said, handing him the gun. "I don't really need it."

⊠ ⊠ ⊠

Nearly five weeks had passed since Dunn came to live hand-to-mouth, sleeping in a youth hostel, relying on the support of his friend Samir, begging his literary agent for petty cash, waiting for resolution that never came. It was an impecunious period of high anxiety for the writer, and in all that time, Dunn heard very little from Interpol. He had telephoned for the return of, if nothing else, his laptop computer. *The least they can do under the circumstances*, Dunn thought. *They've done so little as it is.* He needed his life back. He craved the return to normality. He was in the middle of crafting a pretty damn good novel, despite his predicament, despite having kidnapped a girl and imprisoned her in Samir's basement. He needed his laptop, but Interpol had denied him access to it.

Ever since the kidnapping, he'd managed only fitful snatches of sleep at night for fear of getting arrested and sent to prison. As a writer used to researching the criminal justice system, police procedures, penitentiary life, etc., research for the

Max Sledge Mysteries, he knew nothing about the Dutch prison system. He had no idea what he was facing should he end up there, and as such, his nightmares were full of unpleasant things: the aberrant sexual practices of thick-necked Dutchmen; no one hears you scream in solitary confinement; psychopathic prison guards with a penchant for torture. With the recent addition of red-rimmed eyes and dark circles, along with his unkempt hair and ragged clothes, Dunn looked like a madman. He could no longer pass for a modestly esteemed writer of mystery novels. He looked like a common criminal, a jailbird in training.

That morning, as he slouched through his routine—rising from his bug-infested cot and making his way across the canal to Samir Arslan's restaurant—Dunn was reconciled to his fate of spending the next twenty-years-to-life in prison for the kidnapping of Audrey. At his age, twenty years behind bars was a virtual death sentence. As he eased into his usual chair under the restaurant awning, he decided to set her free that very afternoon, irrespective of the consequences. He could no longer live with himself, with what he had done. The decision was made; his mind was made up.

Looking at the empty tables, he wondered where were the customers. At that hour, Samir's was typically packed with students from the hostel and with locals, downing croissants and espressos, reading copies of *De Telegraaf* and smoking Royal

Dutch cigarettes. But not this day. The place was abandoned.

In the canal a green barge bleated at another filled with produce, maneuvering past like hippopotamuses. As the quiet returned, Dunn thought he heard what sounded like bawling puppies. Shading his brow, he looked inside the restaurant and saw Samir's three daughters in a tableau of tragedy. Their wailing sickened the moist Amsterdam air. Samir was nowhere to be seen.

Dunn shouted through the locked glass doors. "*Girls*, where's your father?!"

The two younger daughters seemed to lose strength in their legs and they tumbled to the floor, their eyes running with tears, mouths agape. The oldest daughter, Atifa (which means *Gift*), unlocked the door. She spoke to her father's strange friend through choking sobs.

"The police, they arrested my father."

Against his better judgment, Dunn asked, "What for, immigration problems or something?"

She shook her head. Samir was being held but Atifa had no idea where, no idea what to do. She was beside herself as she fell to the tiled floor, her sisters wailing like coyotes and beating their chests with fists.

Dunn assured Atifa that he would take care of it. He had a reasonably good hunch what *it* was, but would not tell her. Rather, he would go see the police and arrange Samir's immediate release. "This is just a misunderstanding," he reassured her. "I'll make everything okay. You'll see."

He started off for the local police station at a brisk pace but soon slowed as second thoughts brought him to a stand still beside the canal. Dunn's mind was simplistic, but it didn't take a genius to figure out why the police took Samir into custody. It had nothing to do with his immigration status. Rather, Dunn was reasonably sure, the Druze had taken the toy gun and paid a visit to the Hollis Gang.

And something had gone terribly wrong.

Rather than obtain Dunn's passport and property, Samir was *bushwhacked*, as Max Sledge called it. Stanley and the Greek boy had turned tables on the luckless Druze. Probably called the police that there was an Arab terrorist in the neighborhood with an automatic weapon. They'd arrested him despite the toy gun and charged him with public endangerment, kept him in custody long enough for a background check. Samir would have cooperated, no doubt. No telling whether he would sing in hopes of a quick release, but the song, Dunn knew, would link him to kidnapping and the criminal imprisonment of an "innocent" girl. In other words, Samir would sing the lyrics of betrayal.

There was no way Dunn could go to the police, not now, not with Audrey bound in the basement. For all he knew, at that very moment, the police could be untying her with assurances that the kidnapper would soon be clapped in irons.

He had no choice but to return to the basement and let the girl go now.

Chapter Eight

ODDLY, HE FOUND the backdoor to the basement ajar. The lock appeared tampered with; there were screwdriver marks in the wood. He'd hoped to find things as he'd left them. Now his heart was at his throat in a gallop, and the faint promise of the day went completely sour.

It took all his courage to push open the door and peer down the dark stairs.

"Audrey?" he called. "Everything all right?"

Someone made a muffled reply. Funny, he couldn't remember whether he'd brought a hood and gag on his previous visit.

Dunn came cautiously down the steps to find a scene not too dissimilar to the one Mary Magdalen saw in the Tomb. A loose rope coiled on the floor next to an empty folding chair. Audrey was gone.

He stood stock-still and tried to process what this unfortunate turn of events meant to his longevity.

"Max Sledge."

The disembodied male voice came from behind, from the darkest corner beneath the stairs. Dunn looked but saw no one. He was about to burst with panic.

Another voice spoke in a foreign tongue, harsher, guttural. *Greek*, Dunn thought.

Audrey Klein stepped into the weak light coming from the top of the stairs. She was rubbing her wrist where the ropes had chaffed and she was staring hatefully. That's when Dunn saw the barrel of the nickel-plated gun like the glint of a crucifix in the dark.

"Finally decided to come back, huh?" Audrey said.

She walked right up and cracked him across the face with a shut fist. Someone else punched or kicked him in the stomach and he went down.

He took a hundred blows.

He was bleeding, definitely bleeding. All he saw was blood on the stone floor. He didn't know he had that much blood in him. His face was numb, his nose broken.

"Let me tie him up," Dunn heard Audrey say.

She was rough with him despite his protests and wretched pleading. So now, in addition to his whole head going numb, his hands, cut off from circulation, went dead.

Wearing a fisherman's cap and reeking of patchouli oil, the Greek boy lifted him onto the chair. While Audrey lashed his ankles, Dunn stared into the boy's liquid black eyes. It was like going eye to eye with a killer shark made all the more scary by its efficient detachment.

The last actor in the fright show to come forward was Stanley Gray or Bledsoe. Dunn's head was having difficulty sorting out the names.

He was pointing an enormous revolver with a long barrel, so heavy the kid gripped it in both hands. He grinned crazily with a toothpick between his teeth.

"Since you're gonna ask anyway," Stanley said. "It's a fifty caliber Magnum. Nine inch barrel." He placed his booted foot on the folding chair and leaned down to Dunn's ear. He rested the gun on his knee and removed the toothpick. "Remember that movie when Dirty Harry says, you know, 'This is the most powerful handgun in the world'? Well, mine's bigger." Stanley's eye twitched. "Cut you clean in half, dude."

He reminded the writer of a character from his last novel, the antagonist, a juvenile delinquent serial killer with a rash of acne.

"Look, I don't know what you're doing but…"

Audrey slapped him. "Shut the fuck up!"

It may have had little force behind it but she connected with Dunn's nose and he bolted over in agony.

"Aughh…*please…don't…!*"

Again, with his hot fetid breath in Dunn's face, Stanley said, "What'd you think you were doing, taking my woman like that, huh? Thought you was gonna get some? Tell me. I wanna know, motherfucker."

He pulled back, a dead-serious look on his face, as he leveled the revolver at Dunn's head. Audrey and the Greek boy moved away, not wanting to get blood on their new clothes.

"Tell me before I blow your fuckin' brains all over your fuckin' basement."

Dunn mumbled that it wasn't his basement, not *per se*, he said, wincing for having said it, chastising himself for speaking without thinking, waiting for the next blow to come. Or worse.

Stanley leaned forward. "What'd you say? Speak up, asshole. I can't hear you."

"I said…"

"Louder!"

Dunn swallowed. "I said, this isn't my basement."

Stanley kicked the leg of the folding chair, and Dunn collapsed with it onto the floor, chair and man bound together as a single unit, latent and sacrificial.

"You think we fucking care whose basement this is?"

Audrey whispered something in her boyfriend's ear. "Really?" he said, his features softening vaguely for her sake. Darkening once again, he turned to Dunn.

"Tell me something, Max Sledge. That's your name, ain't it? Am I right? Famous writer of books and shit. Big literary man. Well, I never heard a you." He squared his shoulders as though addressing a crowd and shouted. *"Say, anybody ever hear of this joker?!"* His voice rang like a carillon in the stone room. Stanley laughed and leaned closer. "Since you're so smart, why don't you tell me who owns the basement. Maybe your partner, huh? That fucking towel head?"

Visions of Samir's three daughters raced through Dunn's mind. His betrayal would only bring down more misery on that family, something he would rather die than cause. He said nothing.

He heard the solid metallic click of the trigger and felt the cold steel against his temple.

Dunn had never been one to go to church every Sunday—something his ex-wife Marjorie tried to get him to do—and he didn't much believe in the power of prayer. But in that instant before he was about to die, he tried to remember the Lord's Prayer, hoping by repeating it to earn an express pass into Heaven. His swollen lips moved as he silently recited, "Our Father who art in Heaven…Thy Kingdom come…." *No, that's not right*, he thought and started over. "Our Father who art in Heaven, hallowed be Thy name. Thy Kingdom come, Thy will be done…."

While Dunn made peace with his maker, Stanley's finger pressed against the trigger. He grimaced in anticipation of the explosion sure to follow, as he pulled harder. Nothing. His hands began to sweat because he had never killed a guy before, although he'd bragged to Odysseus (that's what he called the Greek) about shooting two Mexicans in Texas in a bad drug deal. All of it pure bullshit. This was a new experience for him, but he was game to try nonetheless. It might show his woman just how far he was willing to go to prove his love for her. And maybe afterwards when the geezer's brains were splattered all over the place, Audrey might change her flirtatious ways and stick to the plan, give herself to Stanley alone, not even *look* at another dude.

Stanley checked the safety. It was off. Again he squeezed the trigger. And again nothing.

"Goddamnit!"

"What's wrong?" Audrey said.

He waggled the revolver as though to loosen up a malfunctioning part. "Fuckin' thing won't shoot."

"Here," she said, "give it to me."

"No way. This is my gig."

Audrey stepped back, arms akimbo, head cocked aside. "Your gig? How you figure, genius? Who you think was locked up in this fucking room for days, huh?"

"Look, honey…"

"Don't fuckin' *honey* me, Stanley. Give me the goddamned gun."

Reluctantly, he handed over the weapon.

Audrey strained to lift the heavy revolver and pull the trigger.

"Goddammit!"

"Told you so," Stanley said, his tone whiny, almost effeminate.

The Greek said something in his native language, and the girl barked, "What would you suggest, numb-nuts?" The boy shrugged.

"Well, it's obvious. We gotta whack him." Stanley's swaggering macho had returned.

"*Whack* him?" Audrey's mouth was half open, incredulous at her boyfriend's loose grip on reality. "Who're you now, Tony Soprano?"

"What do you suggest, sweetcakes?"

She turned the gun around and handed it back handle first. "Beat him with it. Beat him to death."

Stanley towered over the writer with his arm raised, the double-action revolver held like a hammer by the barrel, hesitating. "Go ahead," Audrey encouraged. "Do it." He flinched and gritted his teeth. "Don't rush me," was all he said.

At this point Dunn had come to terms with getting beaten to death, which he suspected was a drawn-out, painful process. He would have preferred the quicker method of getting shot in the head. At least then you didn't suffer as much as from a beating, which took longer and involved multiple blows. *Oh, I hope they don't hit my nose again*, he was thinking. He shut his eyes and held his breath.

"Do it!" Audrey shouted.

Stanley dropped his arm and gave a defeated sigh. "I hate this shit."

From his motorcycle boots, the Greek pulled a long silvery knife and showed it to the girl. Stanley took one look and said, "No. I hate knives. This is what we're gonna do, okay, dudes. Listen. We take him back to our place and wait till, I don't know, midnight or something. Then when nobody's around, we tie him down in the street and run over him with the Alfa."

"*What?!*" Audrey was again incredulous. "You out of your frickin' mind?"

"Gotta better idea?"

"You think some asshole's not gonna see that? Look, we kill him here...cut his throat or whatever...it's clean. No witnesses. Run him over with the car? What're you, nuts?"

Just then Dunn was remembering the first time he'd met Audrey. She'd put on airs about being a spokesmodel for MSNBC with perfect diction. Now, in this claustrophobic room where he would surely meet his end, he'd detected a Kentucky accent, a nasally mid-west drawl that reminded him of the intermarriages of Appalachia.

Her boyfriend handed her the Smith & Wesson. "Where're you goin', Stanley? You better not be duckin' out on me," she exclaimed.

He was halfway to the door, up the stairs. He turned round. "Keep your panties on, gorgeous. I'm gonna check some things out, is all. Be right back. Sit tight. Hold the gun on the prisoner." And he was gone.

After a while the numbness in Dunn's face was beginning to resolve into searing pain. With his nose swollen shut, he breathed through his mouth, the taste of blood thick on his tongue and in the back of his throat. He recalled passages from one of the Max Sledge Mysteries where his hero endured two or three pages of torture at the hands of social malcontents. What was it that Max had called them, cretin misfits? More importantly, how had he managed to escape? Funny, he was thinking, how the mind wanders aimlessly when you're about to be murdered.

"You happy now, you old fool?"

Dunn looked up to see Audrey balancing the revolver from one hand to the other.

"Can I ask you something?" he said. When she failed to reply, he asked, "How'd you get loose? How did they find you?"

Audrey huffed through her nose in arrogant exasperation. "You're ol' buddy Ahab or whatever, the Arab, he told Stanley and Odysseus here all about your plan. Gave 'em freakin' directions where you was keepin' me. He sold you out."

"Samir?" Dunn was taken aback. His best friend in the world had betrayed him?

"Well…" Audrey smirked. "Not without some persuasion." She gestured with the gun. She crouched in front of the mark and looked him square in the eyes. "Next time you and your camel buddy kidnap a girl, you might want to think about bringing a *real* gun along." She squinted up at him. "Really, dude. It was a toy gun," she said, shaking her head and standing up.

"Would you tell me…?"

"You're gonna have to speak up. I can't hear you."

"Please," Dunn said, "could you tell me what happened to my friend?"

"The Arab?"

Dunn shook his head and the pain made him feel faint. "He's not Arab. He's Druze," he managed to say.

"I don't know. The police got him" was all she said.

Several hours later, Stanley Bledsoe returned with two plastic bags. One contained sandwiches, cigarettes and a six-pack of Heineken. In the other, several clown masks and a red bandanna. Delirious with pain, Dunn thought, *Ah, at least* someone *remembered to bring the gag and hood.*

"Hollis made some sandwiches," Stanley said. "She's tired of waiting."

Audrey and the Greek ate the sandwiches. They offered Dunn nothing, taunting him by grinning as they chewed. It was like watching predators with a fresh kill. Afterwards, they lit up and filled the confining room with cigarette smoke. Stanley popped one of the beers and took a hit of foam off the mouth. "So, has shithead misbehaved or what?" He approached Dunn whose eyes had gone bloodshot. Gripping his thin hair, he wrenched back his head. "He's not lookin' so hot."

"May I have some water?"

"No!" Audrey shouted, crushing her cigarette. "Absolutely not. No fuckin' water for him. Kept me here for days. No food, no water. You want a drink, old man?" She swaggered the bottle of beer in front of him. "You ain't getting any."

"Okay, come on. Enough of this. Put the masks on," Stanley said. "We're gonna walk him back to our place."

"In broad daylight?" the girl asked.

"Nobody'll suspect a bunch a clowns. Anybody stops us, tell 'em it's a masquerade ball or something." He laughed.

"And the bandanna?"

"I want him gagged," Stanley said. "You can cut his ropes now, Odysseus."

At once outside, Dunn felt the warm flush of a low-lying sun, even through the clown mask. It was luxuriant. The Greek boy stood behind him with his knife, and when Dunn hesitated, lifting his chin like a heliotrope, he nicked the old dude's flesh with the blade.

"Move," Audrey scoffed.

It was hard for Dunn to see. In the basement, Stanley had taken the time to adjust everyone's mask to conceal their identity before adjusting his own. But when it came time for the prisoner, Stanley was slapdash. The eyeholes failed to line up, and so Dunn was forced to look through the clown's nostrils, which gave him a peculiar gait. A bit like Quasimodo. Breathing was an altogether different challenge. Just moments earlier, he had tried to explain that his nose was blocked by dried blood and that he needed his mouth free to breathe, but they gagged him anyway. Now Poor Dunn was circling the drain of hypoxia.

Stanley acted the field marshal by hanging back from the parade of clowns. "I got our insurance," he told Audrey, patting the bulge in his waistband. "Someone fucks with us, I'll take care of it." She didn't have the patience to remind him once again, the Magnum was defective. He seemed more field mouse than field marshal, in a position to run away if it came to that.

The Greek, by comparison, was enjoying himself having adapted well to the mask. He smoked cigarettes that he fit in the mouth hole. Stanley would have objected had he caught him at it. In his opinion, smoking violated the very essence of what it meant to be a clown. You never saw Ronald McDonald smoking a cigarette; this was how Stanley's mind worked.

As they walked casually down De Wittenkade for Fannius Scholtenstraat, their first test came when a young couple in leathers and chains approached. The guy, obviously stoned, danced around them like a Maypole, cigarette stuck in his gap-toothed grin. He laughed and whooped like a hyena while his multiple-pierced girlfriend with a face full of tattoos withdrew to the canal because the clowns were freaking her out. Eventually, Stanley had to walk up and tell him, "*Easy, Dude!* Hello, don't be so dorky."

The Greek ushered Dunn away, and without looking, led him right into a lamppost. The sound it made inside Dunn's head was like the dull clang of a cracked bell. He was on his back, unsure of how he'd gotten there, as Audrey and the Greek stood him up. "You all right?" the girl asked. They took either arm, and the three proceeded in tandem.

Next came an elderly couple pushing a tram full of groceries. They scowled in disapproval. It was Audrey's turn to show the colors. In her best juvenile delinquent, she intoned, "Yeah, like you never did this." When the couple felt threatened, she laughed for the first time that day. She lifted the mask so its face was on top of her head and she asked the Greek for a cigarette. When Stanley shouted, "Put the mask on!" Audrey turned and flipped him both barrels. "Eat me," she said.

Not far from Samir's, the Greek noticed two hookers standing under the awning. The restaurant was still closed. One hooker wore a blonde wig, the other a metallic red one. They figured the clowns for tourists, American college students on a bender. "Do all three," the blonde said. "Fifty guilders."

Here was something to pique Audrey's interest. "Guilders?"

The redhead waved her hands. "She mean euros. *Each!*"

"Let's party," the blonde said.

Audrey laughed. "I'm a girl."

Both hookers nodded. "She know dat," the redhead said.

The clowns moved down the straat just as the lamps were coming on. The barges strung with Christmas lights added to the Amsterdam atmosphere of festive vitality, necklaces of color reflecting in the canal like oil paint. The sun had dipped below the horizon, bringing on an evening where the sky was brighter than the city streets and shuttered shops. As the clown parade approached the bridge close to their apartment, it seemed to Stanley that someone was following them.

More than once he'd quickly turned around because of the crunch of shoes coming from behind. But each time he'd looked, nobody was there. It made him nervous, but then again, everything made him nervous. He'd spent much of his young life concealing a nervous disposition from the world.

Stanley wasn't one to put on a front like some dudes did, but being jumpy, which was his natural state, didn't seem to fit the personality of a petty crook. Weren't criminals supposed to act cool, like in the movies? He was thinking Brad Pitt in *Ocean's Eleven* and that stone cold killer in *No Country for Old Men*. That's how he fancied himself, aloof, indifferent to a victim's cries, a steady hand and sharp eye.

There it was again, that sound of shoe leather on cobblestones.

This time Stanley pulled his weapon. Maybe whoever it was would see the nickel plating in the dark and back off.

The figure of a man in a trench coat moved out of the darkness. Two other men, broad at the shoulder and taller, stood behind like twin shadows.

The trench coat spoke. "Are you sure you want to take eet this far, Monsieur?"

Whoever he was, Stanley considered the accent unusual for Amsterdam but was unable to identify it. He thought, maybe the man was French.

"Back off, dude," he said.

"You're making a beeg mistake."

Squinting through darkness, Stanley saw the flash of something in the figure's hand, a bronze shield like a cop would wear.

"Stop in zee name of Interpol. You are under arrest."

Stanley bolted. In a few seconds he'd caught up with the clown parade just as they reached the top of the canal bridge.

The Interpol officers came running in pursuit with the trench coat blowing a whistle. "Alt!" they shouted. "Alt."

Two white police cars, sirens wailing, blue lights flashing, pulled up to block the intersection. The officers jumped out and drew their weapons, trapping them.

The four clowns on the bridge stood looking from one impediment to the other. The Greek weighed what his chances were over the railing, in the canal. Stanley couldn't stand still for his nerves. He wished he'd thought about peeing before they'd left the basement, but now it was too late.

Audrey had had enough frustration for one day and grabbed Stanley's Smith & Wesson .50 caliber Magnum and brandished it, shouting gutturally to be heard above the sirens, telling the cops to back off or she'd blow "this motherfucker away."

Dunn had not seen very much of the proceedings, but from what he could tell, he was in deep. Audrey had him in a headlock with the revolver pointed at the back of his head. She screamed something, details of which were lost on account of the racking pains shooting through his skull. His beating heart sounded like a kettledrum. He was close to passing out. In fact, he wished he had. As far as Dunn was concerned, the whole month had been an ordeal. He just wished, like Dorothy in *The Wizard of Oz*, that he could click his heels and go home, sit in his townhouse study and work on another Max Sledge Mystery. He was fantasizing about how nice it would be, sitting there alone with his stories, sipping a cup of tea, just as Audrey and he spun around to face the man in the trench coat.

"Don't make me pull the trigger!" she shouted.

"Put zee gun down, Mademoiselle."

Audrey cocked the weapon. The weight of it pressed against the back of Dunn's head.

"Eet is over, Mademoiselle. Your leetle schemes. It is finished. How you say in American, *kaput?*"

Dunn mumbled into his gag, "'*erman!*" and wished he hadn't.

"Shut up, asshole." Audrey tightened her grip on his neck.

In the midst of the confusion, Dunn heard a familiar voice calling above the wailing police sirens. *Robert*, the voice said, *Robert, all is well. No worries, my friend. Allah protected us.* Whoever it was, they shouted from inside a police car and waved hysterically out the back window. The person was smiling so broadly, Dunn saw only the shine of white teeth.

"'amir?"

"Told you to shut up." Audrey knocked the barrel of the gun against his skull.

"Put zee weapon down, Mademoiselle. This is your last warning."

Something had just occurred to Dunn, an idea in the middle of all the pain rising to the top of his bruised mind like a gigantic trout in a lake. It had something to do with the revolver, that it didn't work very well. *Isn't that why they didn't shoot me earlier?* The idea clarified, as it would have in Max Sledge's mind. There wasn't anything to worry about. The tables were turned. Audrey couldn't shoot him because the enormous gun was impotent.

At that moment, Dunn stood up straight and with all his strength grabbed the gun from Audrey's sweat-slick hands. When she yelled at him, he shoved her and she fell down on her perfectly sculpted bum, ripping her Spandex, the clown mask sliding around her neck.

In a languid move—cool, debonair, and make-believe—Max Sledge tossed the revolver over the bridge railing. A moment later, everyone heard the significant splash of it dropping into the canal.

Chapter Nine

AFTER SPENDING SEVERAL days in the hospital, Bob Dunn sat across from Inspector Valadon in his office at Interpol.

"Here is your passport. Zee good one. You may leave Amsterdam anytime you weesh. No more youth hostel, eh?" The inspector smiled. "And now you can use *la studette*. The apartment, she is free." The American was deadpan, the epitome of gauche. "*Redouter l'ironie, c'est craindre la raison...?*"

His nose plastered by a surgical bandage the size of a tennis ball, Bob Dunn offered a polite smile. Valadon winced sympathetically at the man's discomfort. When he and his officers had removed Dunn's clown mask on the night of the arrests, he recalled registering shock. The upper lip was horribly swollen, eyes blackened and the nose beyond recognition as a nose. At the hands of his captors, the American writer had suffered a great deal.

Dunn fought the urge to scratch his injuries beneath the bandages. He'd been eyeing a cup of blue pencils on Valadon's desk with the idea of sticking the eraser end beneath the gauze to give his nose a good daubing. He played with a prescription bottle of pain medication in his pants pocket. He wasn't sure what kind they were, but they did the trick. Made him a little fuzzy though. Half the things the inspector said, Dunn didn't pay much attention to or understand.

Inspector Valadon was very pleased with himself, and it showed. He couldn't stop smiling. He'd been such a chatterbox all morning, which was unlike him. There was no longer the need to act the Interpol official, not with the American. The case was closed. During the inspector's brief tenure in the Netherlands, he'd cracked an international identity theft ring and brought most of the perpetrators to justice. In addition, his time served in the Netherlands was coming to an end. Soon, he would return to civilization, back to France, a country that knew how to bake croissants and brew a decent espresso.

Making preparations for his departure, all that remained was to clear out the desk and remove a few personal items from the Interpol apartment. He reflected dreamily on the prospect of seeing his wife and children again, and his mistress, in Lyons. He smiled because he had more to look forward to than simply a warm homecoming—a commendation and a promotion were in the offing. The American writer and his friend, a Lebanese émigré, had played a minor role in solving the criminal case, it was true, and they deserved some credit, but there was the kidnapping to consider and the forced imprisonment, although any and all charges had been dropped in consideration for the gravity of the case. It was front-page news, made all the major papers. Valadon had even been interviewed by CNN. He expected, when he stood at attention on the awards dais next year, the Executive Directorate of Police Services would likely pin the Chevalier de la Legion d'Honneur to his lapel.

"And now," he said, "*pièce de résistance.*" With élan, Valadon removed an official bank document from a Manila folder and presented it across the desk. "*Laisser le meilleur pour la fin.* I leave the best for last." He could not stop smiling.

It was a casino-green cashier's check made out to R. Dunn, issued by Credit Suisse for €13,395.

Dunn looked past the bandages at the inspector. "You got my money back?"

Valadon bobbed his head enthusiastically. "Zee bad guys, they had a bank account. Here in Amsterdam."

Dunn picked up the check. "There must be some mistake."

"*Non.* No mistake, I assure you, Monsieur." He glanced down at the case paperwork, ignoring the fickle American. "You weel have minor loses, of course. Zee Italian car. *Carte de crédit.*" He clicked his tongue and looked up.

Dunn returned the check. "By my own calculation…and I think we agreed my figures are correct…Hollis stole *twenty thousand* dollars."

Valadon folded his hands beneath his chin and smiled. "*Oui…*" Nothing was going to spoil his good mood, not even the irrational complaints of the American.

"This check is for…thirteen thousand. A third less."

"Euro's, Monsieur. *Euros!* At zee exchange rate this morning..." Inspector Valadon's fingers danced happily on a calculator and struck the enter key. "Exactly twenty thousand doll-airs. You must be pleased, Monsieur. Interpol deed very well, non?" He handed him the check and arched an eyebrow inquisitively.

Dunn folded it into his billfold. "Thank you, Inspector. I appreciate it."

"Interpol at your service."

"May I ask you one thing before I go, Inspector?"

"But of course."

"Hollis McAllister, the girl who..." Dunn hesitated. How should he phrase it?

He ran a slender finger delicately down a list of names in the file. "Holister Ehrlich?"

"Yes, Holister. Any word on her?"

Valadon shook his head. He was a little disappointed in this minor detail. "She got away, Monsieur. You cannot win zem all."

"Well...she was the brightest of the bunch."

"And beautiful...?"

Dunn gave a slight nod to his hazy head.

"*L'on est bien faible quand on est amoureux, non?*" It was obvious, Valadon had expected a reply, but his clever proverb fell flat with the writer. He closed the Manila file on his desk. "So, you go home now, back to America?"

Dunn nodded solemnly.

"*Le loup retourne toujours au bois.* Au revoir."

"Yes. Au revoir, Inspector."

⊠   ⊠   ⊠

That evening, Samir's three daughters threw a small party for Bob Dunn at the restaurant—food, wine, the works. Atifa Arslan kissed Dunn three times when he showed up, a case of wine in his arms and a bouquet. "These are for you," he told the young woman. Atifa put the flowers in a ceramic vase on the bar. The restaurant was closed but full of family friends and well-wishers, some the writer recognized as regulars. An elegantly trim woman in a black cocktail dress and pearls, said, "Hallo. I must say, you are looking much more well than last time we saw each other."

It was true. After leaving Interpol, Dunn had spent the day shopping and at a health spa for a massage, facial ("Don't touch the nose!") and haircut. His outfit, lavender slacks and silk shirt, casual sports coat and a pair of Berluti shoes, was a vast improvement. None of the accoutrement, however, could divert attention from his bandaged nose.

"I hardly recognized you," the woman said.

When Dunn presented the mixed case of wine to Samir, his old friend wept. He had spent a small fortune on rare French and Italian wines. Samir took great pleasure in exclaiming the names of each as he lifted the bottles. "Côte de Nuits! Ah, *vin jaune!* You remembered, eh? Château latour…!" And on it went until the last. "Alto Adige, Amarone!"

"Well, it's the least I could do," Dunn said. "You were so generous with me...a token of our friendship."

With tears in his eyes, the Druze kissed Dunn on the cheeks and hugged him. Into his ear he said, "We are brothers always, you and I."

Between seven courses and endless bottles of wine—a delicious Pinot Nero from Montepulciano—and boisterous conversation that eventually ended in Lebanese folk songs (Dunn hummed along), the old friends managed to sneak off for cigarettes at an outside table, to talk.

Samir plunked down two glasses of Port on the table and brushed the wet leaves from a pair of bistro chairs. "Here, sit. Let us talk," he said. "Away from the craziness."

The party inside was in full swing. They drank their Port as they had always done and smoked one cigarette apiece. Atifa looked through the glass doors and said, "Papa, you promised." Her father called back, "Just this one, I swear."

"Samir," Dunn said at last, "there's something I've been meaning to ask."

"Yes, go ahead. Anything." He took a pleasurable drag on the cigarette.

"The night the police arrested you, what happened? You never told me."

"Well..." Samir smiled to himself. "I do what I tell you. With my son's toy pistol, I stop those *Ghabans* on street, outside apartment. You know it." He stood now to act out his role in what had happened. "I hold gun like this and when they come up, I curl my lip, just like John Wayne. 'You don't know who you are dealing with,' I say to them. But they got the jump…how do you call it?"

"You mean *bushwhacked?*"

"Yes, they whacked-bush me." Samir sat down and crushed the cigarette. "The skinny one, you know him? With the skin like orange peel."

"With the acne."

"Yes. He took out biggest gun Samir see entire life." He lifted the Port and tossed it back. "Almost wet my pantaloons."

"What happened next?"

"The skinny one, tell me, 'Where girlfriend?' Sorry, my friend, I sing like Canary Islands. Tell everything. Still, the *Ghaban*, he point big gun at Samir. He going kill me." He shrugged affably. "But what you know, he no shoot. I run. No more John Wayne."

"You could've been shot."

"I know it, but Allah is merciful. He no shoot. I run for life. I run in the night. I run into a policeman. Knock him over. I try apologize but he see my toy pistol. Samir go to jail." He shook another cigarette from the pack and put a match to it. "No tell Atifa." He exhaled a cloud of smoke. "I confess, but I no say nothing about kidnapping. I give you name, Robert Dunn. Tell police everything, Hollis Gang, how they stole you money. Everything."

"And they believed you."

"Yes. Yes. In morning, Frenchman…what you call him? He come to jail. Ask me show where they live. I show him. Police put up, how you say, stake out." Samir shrugged. "Boom. End a story."

The evening came to a close with the revelers walking off in pairs along the canals for their homes and apartments. Dunn was the last to leave. "Where you staying?" Samir asked. The Steigenberger Kurhaus. Samir gestured that the hotel was pricey. "It's nicer than the youth hostel," Dunn said. Atifa called for a cab, and when it arrived, promises were made at the door, addresses and phone numbers in America written down. A long good-bye outside, on the terrace beneath the awning. Their friend, the American writer of mysterious books, waved a little sadly as the cab pulled away in the night.

It was beginning to rain. Dunn was happy for it. "They won't see my tears this way," he said quietly in the back of the car.

✉ ✉ ✉

His travel agent had provided a meticulous itinerary for his trip back to the States. Direct flight out of Schiphol to Heathrow, from there to Kennedy and SFO, twenty-two hours with three layovers. In the hotel the following day, Dunn ate a room-service breakfast and stared at the tickets. The flight out of Amsterdam to London took off in a few hours. He weighed his options while sipping coffee from a porcelain cup. There were no options. His laptop and luggage, the suitcase of books—all returned by Interpol unmolested—everything was tidy in a corner and waiting for the bellhop. When the knock came at the door, Dunn stood and said, "This isn't going to work." He told the bellhop that he had changed his mind, that he would be staying a few extra days, and he handed to him five euro coins for his trouble.

He opened the laptop and connected quickly to the Internet, toggling down a list of luxury liners and their ports-of-call. As luck would have it, the Queen Mary 2 was leaving in two days. He telephoned an agency listed on the Website and was delighted to learn that a first class suite was available. "I must say, at considerable price," the British agent said. Dunn told her to book it. "And how will you be paying for your crossing, sir?" He told her to expect to receive this afternoon a cashier's check from Credit Suisse made out to their agency. "That should cover it, sir," she said. "Will there be anything else?" Dunn booked a London hotel and asked if they provided shuttle service from the hotel to Southampton. "Yes, sir, we do. In your case, it's complimentary. But it's not a shuttle." The limousine would pick him up promptly at six in the morning before the ship sailed. Dunn thanked the agent and hung up.

The crossing took six days and was entirely—gratefully—uneventful. It gave Dunn time to write undisturbed. He spent most days in the suite, primarily to work on his new novel but secondarily to avoid having to explain his nose bandages to the other passengers. He ordered meals when hungry and bottles of Champagne when he was thristy, but he worked harder than he had ever before. He was writing something completely new. And it didn't involve Max Sledge. "This ought to knock the knickers off Ms. Felicity Jane," he told himself. "Just what the doctor ordered."

It was about an Italian inspector working for Interpol out of Milan. The character's name was Ernesto Bandolini, fashioned after Emile Valadon but without the French accent and aphorisms. The plot involved a widower, an insurance claims adjuster from Ann Arbor, traveling on the Northern Star to Europe. Dunn pretty much followed his own story to the letter, filling in details of casual acquaintances and new-made friends, the members of the Hollis Gang, but, of course, he made sure to change everyone's name for the sake of propriety.

Near the end of the crossing, Dunn completed the first draft, and he sent it via satellite link to his agent in New York, along with an email note:

> *Glenda Darling,*
> *I have taken the QM2 out of Southampton and will arrive early tomorrow. Cannot tell you how thrilled I am to be coming home! To feel so alive again is a feeling beyond my ability to describe as a writer. Speaking of which, I've attached my latest. You might be surprised. It is something completely new for me. Let me know what you think when I see you.*

Also, my good friend, I have not had a chance to thank you (soon, I'll have that chance) for what you did for me in my time of trial. You were an angel, truly. Of course, I will repay you in full and more. Let me take you to Sardi's for dinner, my treat.

I am not fully recovered from the effects of this fiasco. In fact, my features have been rearranged. I have the schnoz of Rocky Marciano. So, please, no theatrics when you first lay eyes on me in NYC.

You shall see that the threads of my adventures during the Atlantic crossing and in Europe are faithfully woven into the novel. I hope you adore it because it nearly cost me my life.

All my love, Bobby

Two months later during negotiations with the publisher, Dunn decided to drop the pseudonym Ashley Winslow. When *The Crossing* by Robert H. Dunn came out in hardback, it received a passionate appraisal in *The New York Times Book Review*, and sales blew the knickers off his editor, Ms. Felicity Jane. Thereafter, she was obligated to act graciously, if somewhat reluctantly, in her dealings with the author. After the paperback was released, there was talk of a movie with Roberto Benigni in the title role. Dunn couldn't have been more pleased with his literary success, but still, something was missing in his life.

Dunn kept his townhouse in Vacaville, despite the fact that he could have purchased a nicer home. Instead, he bought a five-room cabin on the Sonoma coast. During the middle of the week, he would often drive up Highway One in his new Italian sports car, an Alfa Romeo. Since he'd already paid for another one that he never had the pleasure to drive, he wanted to see what the hoopla was all about. The car didn't disappoint.

✉   ✉   ✉

In early March of the following year, after a long recovery from nose surgery, Dunn was at home, writing into the night. It was what he enjoyed, uninterrupted hours to work on the third novel in the Ernesto Bandolini Series. This one involved the kidnapping of a Lebanese girl. He was scheduled to fly to Amsterdam in the next month to visit Samir and his daughters, for "research."

Dunn was lost in thought when the doorbell rang.

Half-past nine was far too late to entertain guests. "Probably someone from the Vacaville Women's Literary League." He hoped they would take the hint that he wasn't in the mood to see anyone. Sill, he didn't want to be rude and lose a fan.

He checked the hallway mirror. He was presentable with his Hemingway cachet of ten-day old stubble. The doorbell rang again.

"Coming," he called.

To say that he was stunned does not even remotely approach his reaction to seeing Hollis at the door.

Had he not been so fraught with doubt that she could possibly be standing there, he would have noticed the gun.

"Hollis?"

That's when he noticed it.

Without a word she stepped over the threshold and shut the door behind her, almost seductively it seemed to Dunn. She wore a beige London Fog and had on the pair of Jackie Kennedy sunglasses he'd bought for her in Venice.

"Your hair's different."

"Are you alone?"

"No one here." He gave it a second thought. "Just the two of us."

She motioned with the firearm to walk ahead of her into the main room of the house.

"What is that?" Dunn asked.

"A gun, you idiot."

"No, I mean, what make? It's beautiful somehow."

"A Beretta nine-fifty Jetfire," Hollis said.

"Suits you."

She commanded that he sit. Dunn took his favorite chair while Hollis stood in the middle of the room, legs apart and weapon to the fore. Nothing was said for a time, the present circumstances not prone to polite conversation, and so he launched a trial balloon.

"You're looking well."

"Shut up—"

"Please, Hollis...may I call you *Hollis*? Or would you prefer Holister?" Dunn asked, leaning forward and chaffing his hands. "If I'm correct in saying these next few minutes are going to be my last, I think I deserve to know why, don't you?"

She said nothing. It was hard to know what she was thinking behind the preposterously wide sunglasses.

"How did you find me?" he asked.

"I know everything about you. I stole your identity, remember?"

Dunn was considering for the moment, had she been intent on killing him, he already would have been dead by now.

"Why are you here, Hollis?"

She huffed. "Isn't it obvious?"

"I'd like to hear you say it."

That got to her. She shifted her center of gravity and took a wobbly step back on the carpet. Dunn noticed that she wore black stiletto pumps, something the femme fatale's in his novels should have worn.

"You ruined my life," she said, "you bastard."

"How have I ruined your life? You're here, aren't you? Last time I checked, your buddies are doing hard time in a Dutch prison."

"Fucking Interpol stole my money. I had a fortune."

"Stolen from men like me."

Up to this point, she more or less held the pistol in Dunn's general direction. But his remark pissed her off, and she raised the Beretta at his head.

"Look, what I mean is," he began. "I don't think your friends are suffering a great deal in that Dutch prison. It's not the Langham, for sure." He hoped she would remember. "But it isn't Devil's Island either." His appeal to reason wasn't getting through. "Look, at least let's have one last drink together before you...*do* what you've come to do. Can I make you a drink? I know I'd like one."

Hollis felt indecisive for a beat or two.

Dunn lifted his arms in expectation of an answer. "Mother, may I get up and fix drinks at the wet bar?"

"Okay." She followed him closely. "Don't do anything stupid."

"What, throw ice cubes at you?" He selected a large cocktail glass and poured a healthy serving of Scotch, taken neat.

"Is that a Macallan?"

Dunn waggled the bottle. "Confirmed. Would you like a shot or two?"

"That's pretty expensive stuff."

"I'd be lying if I said it could be easily had at the corner liquor store. Cost me over a thousand bucks.

I'll be damned if I'm going to die without getting good and drunk on it."

He presented the cocktail. An awkward moment passed in which she couldn't decide to use her left or right hand. Dunn sat back in his chair and took a hearty gulp. "Won't you sit down?" He sipped the whisky. "God, this is glorious." Feeling the liquor's heat, he smiled. "Perhaps we should toast something?" He raised his glass. She ignored the taunt. "To being reunited. You've never looked more beautiful." Dunn drained the glass and had some trouble rising out of the chair. "If you don't mind, I'll pour myself another."

As she watched him at the wet bar, his back to her, she tasted the whisky. It was ambrosia.

"Hollis." Dunn returned to the chair with another cocktail and the bottle that he carefully placed on a coaster within reach. "Hollis, Hollis, Hollis."

She might have smiled ever so faintly.

He took a drink and glanced at his wristwatch. "How much time do we have?"

"What're you going on about?"

"Well, I mean, before you shoot me. I'd like to know how much longer I have. Approximately speaking." He tippled the whisky.

"Shut up, Max."

He shook his head. "No, that won't do. Max Sledge, the man you knew before…that would be me…is no longer. I did away with him." He giggled. "Look at that. We have something in common."

"What do you mean?"

God, is she that dense?

"By that, I mean, doing away with someone, we have that in common. You see, I did away with...never mind. Anyway, Max Sledge is dead. I killed him."

"I'll call you Ashley then."

"Nope," Dunn said, his lips having gone numb. "Ashley Winslow also bit the dust. Took a powder. Went to the happy hunting grounds. Beyond the grave. Snuffed out. Kicked the bucket. Breathed his last..."

"Would you please stop."

"Hollis, if you kill me, you'll be ending your life."

She huffed. "Maybe. But you'll be dead."

He focused through imperfect vision. She glowed. "Don't do this for your own sake. Honestly, I don't care about me, not really. I'm old, washed up, venerable, long in the tooth, one foot in the grave...well, you get the idea." Dunn raised his glass to her. "Sorry, but Scotch loosens the writer in me."

"Give me one good reason why I shouldn't kill you."

"Well," Dunn considered. "I've already given you several reasons, haven't I? I mean, if you'd been listening..."

She removed the sunglasses and stuffed them in the pocket of the trench coat.

There came the distinct sound of a thumb pulling back the hammer of a pistol, a Beretta Jetfire. Dunn sighed. "So, it would seem, I've overstayed my welcome."

She still hadn't shot him, and he thought he might have a chance.

"Hollis, before I die I must tell you, I did truly love you." His voice cracked. "You're going to laugh, but after my wife left, I wasn't exactly Lothario with the ladies. In fact, you could say your old pal was a stick in the mud. I see you smiling, yes. I can be a stick in the mud, can't I? I mean, that time we checked into the *palazzo* in Venice, remember? When that awful lady called you my *belissima* daughter. I didn't defend you. I know, I should have. It wasn't fair of me at all. Should have pushed the old bat in the *canali*."

The sound of a laugh escaped from her and she hated herself for it, stiffened and put more pressure on the trigger. What was she waiting for? It was ridiculous to listen to the old man. She should have just shot him in the doorway and been done with it when she had the chance. Now, with all his talking and nonsense, she'd probably end up crying in her rental car on her way to the airport, regretting the whole episode.

"You were the best thing that ever happened to me," Dunn said.

"Then why…why did you turn us in?" She had a desperate look in her eye with the sliver of tragic affection for the old man.

"Hollis, you stole twenty thousand dollars from me. I mean, it isn't every day one takes a cruise, meets the most beautiful girl in the world and gets fucking ripped off, if you'll pardon the expression."

Because he never used profanity, they laughed together in a kind of *pas de deux* full of reconciliation.

"Hollis, if you kill me, the police will hunt you down. I know, darling, because I've been writing stories about this kind of thing my entire life. Crime doesn't pay. It just doesn't."

For the first time since she'd forced her way into his townhouse, she lowered the weapon. Dunn was thinking, if he survived the next few minutes, later he'd definitely pray sincerely to one of the gods, Allah or Jesus perhaps.

"If you leave now, Hollis…or even if you decide to stay…" He shrugged. She wasn't buying it. "You're perfectly safe with me. I won't call the police—"

"Why not," she barked.

"Because…" Dunn swallowed the tightness in his throat. "Because, I still love you. No matter what you've done."

"What happened to your nose?" She smirked.

"Don't laugh. Audrey hit me."

"You got that from a *girl?*" She was incredulous.

"You have no idea how many surgeries I've been through to fix it…"

"Does it hurt?" she asked. Her question threw sunlight across the room.

"Well, yeah. Hurts like hell. But honestly, it was worth it." He laughed, and so did she. "You are the best thing that ever happened to me."

That was it, his complete load. He had nothing left. If, after confessing his devotion to her, she'd weighed the appeal and found it deficient, at this point there was nothing more he had to offer. He'd laid out the facts as he saw them, as sincerely as he possibly could. Everything he'd said came from the heart, pure and unencumbered. Emotion laced his every word because that was how he felt, period. Hollis had forced him to open the deepest emotional vaults of his being. If she rejected him, considering the Scotch, the late hour and how drunk he was, he wasn't sure he cared.

"If I leave," she began. "If I go now, you won't call the cops?"

He shook his head. "Never. I'd rather die than betray you. If you don't believe me…" He gestured at the box of books on the floor next to the television. "It's a second edition, I'm afraid. Go ahead, take one."

Hollis picked up the thin hardbound book and read the title, *The Crossing*.

"Open it. Read the dedication," Dunn said.

She did so.

To Hollis, wherever you are. With appreciation.

Without a word, she turned on her beautiful heels and clicked across the tiles at the front door, gripping the book and the gun. Dunn watched from the chair because his legs refused to work.

With her hand on the door handle, she gazed back, perhaps remembering that he'd not been such a bad mark after all. That he'd been fatherly, gentle and kind. In a word, loving. Something Holister Ehrlich had had very little of in her life.

"I'll probably hate myself in the morning, for not shooting you." She smiled.

"Well…" Dunn weighed his options. "You can always come back tomorrow, and we could talk about it."

What vestiges of hatred were left in the room, and in her, vanished in an instant, and were replaced by a sense of change and possibility, emotions she was not altogether comfortable with. Still, here was something she thought she might learn to live with.

"Good-bye," she said. She opened the door and walked out of his life.

Bob Dunn stayed seated in his favorite chair, gripping a sweating cocktail glass half-full of expensive Scotch. He took a breath. It wasn't every day a gorgeous girl walked into his townhouse to threaten him with homicide.

After a time, he willed himself to stand, tottering from the alcohol, gripping the back of the wingback chair. He took baby steps toward the front door. It was still ajar. With the flat of his hand he pushed it closed. He kept his hand there to feel remnants of her for the last time.

Before he returned to his study, he made certain the door was locked.

C. Marcus Parr

About The Author

C. Marcus Parr lives with his wife on a small Oregon farm. His short fiction, poems, and cartoons have appeared in literary magazines and independent press in the United States and Canada. He received the Nancy Pickard Fiction Award, and was runner-up for the Pearl Fiction Award. His short story "The Devil Visits Confidence" was nominated for the Pushcart Prize. His poems "Oppenheimer's Laugh" and "A Thousand Endless Words" were also nominated for a Pushcart.

C. Marcus Parr

www.ingramcontent.com/pod-product-compliance
Lightning Source LLC
Chambersburg PA
CBHW020623250626
47154CB00004B/1631